The Paying Guest

George Gissing

1895

Table of Contents

The Paying Guest

George Gissing

Kessinger Publishing reprints thousands of hard–to–find books!

Visit us at http://www.kessinger.net

CHAPTER I

It was Mumford who saw the advertisement and made the suggestion. His wife gave him a startled look.

'But — you don't mean that it's necessary? Have we been extrav——'

'No, no! Nothing of the kind. It just occurred to me that some such arrangement might be pleasant for you. You must feel lonely, now and then, during the day, and as we have plenty of room——'

Emmeline took the matter seriously, but, being a young woman of some discretion, did not voice all her thoughts. The rent was heavy: so was the cost of Clarence's season–ticket. Against this they had set the advantage of the fine air of Sutton, so good for the child and for the mother, both vastly better in health since they quitted London. Moreover, the remoteness of their friends favoured economy; they could easily decline invitations, and need not often issue them. They had a valid excuse for avoiding public entertainments — an expense so often imposed by mere fashion. The house was roomy, the garden delightful. Clarence, good fellow, might be sincere in his wish for her to have companionship; at the same time, this advertisement had probably appealed to him in another way.

'A YOUNG LADY desires to find a home with respectable, well–connected family, in a suburb of London, or not more than 15 miles from Charing Cross. Can give excellent references. Terms not so much a consideration as comfort and pleasant society. No boarding–house. — Address: Louise, Messrs. Higgins Co., Fenchurch St., E.C.'

She read it again and again. 'It wouldn't be nice if people said that we were taking lodgers.'

'No fear of that. This is evidently some well–to–do person. It's a very common arrangement nowadays, you know; they are called "paying guests." Of course I shouldn't dream of having anyone you didn't thoroughly like the look of.'

'Do you think,' asked Emmeline doubtfully, 'that we should quite do? "Well–connected family"——'

'My dear girl! Surely we have nothing to be ashamed of?'

'Of course not, Clarence. But — and "pleasant society." What about that?'

'Your society is pleasant enough, I hope,' answered Mumford, gracefully. 'And the Fentimans——'

This was the only family with whom they were intimate at Sutton. Nice people; a trifle sober, perhaps, and not in conspicuously flourishing circumstances; but perfectly presentable.

'I'm afraid—' murmured Emmeline, and stopped short. 'As you say,' she added presently, 'this is someone very well off. "Terms not so much a consideration"——'

'Well, I tell you what — there can be no harm in dropping a note. The kind of note that commits one to nothing, you know. Shall I write it, or will you?'

They concocted it together, and the rough draft was copied by Emmeline. She wrote a very pretty hand, and had no difficulty whatever about punctuation. A careful letter, calculated for the eye of refinement; it supplied only the indispensable details of the writer's position, and left terms for future adjustment.

'It's so easy to explain to people,' said Mumford, with an air of satisfaction, when he came back from the post, 'that you wanted a companion. As I'm quite sure you do. A friend coming to stay with you for a time — that's how I should put it.'

A week passed, and there came no reply. Mumford pretended not to care much, but Emmeline imagined a new anxiety in his look.

'Do be frank with me, dear,' she urged one evening. 'Are we living too——'

He answered her with entire truthfulness. Ground for serious uneasiness there was none whatever; he could more than make ends meet, and had every reason to hope it would always be so; but it would relieve his mind if the end of the year saw a rather larger surplus. He was now five-and-thirty — getting on in life. A man ought to make provision beyond the mere life-assurance — and so on.

'Shall I look out for other advertisements?' asked Emmeline.

'Oh, dear, no! It was just that particular one that caught my eye.'

Next morning arrived a letter, signed 'Louise E. Derrick.' The writer said she had been waiting to compare and think over some two hundred answers to her advertisement. 'It's really too absurd. How can I remember them all? But I liked yours as soon as I read it, and I am writing to you first of all. Will you let me come and see you? I can tell you about myself much better than writing. Would tomorrow do, in the afternoon? Please telegraph yes or no to Coburg Lodge, Emilia Road, Tulse Hill.'

The Paying Guest

To think over this letter Mumford missed his ordinary train. It was not exactly the kind of letter he had expected, and Emmeline shared his doubts. The handwriting seemed just passable; there was no orthographic error; but — refinement? This young person wrote, too, with such singular nonchalance. And she said absolutely nothing about her domestic circumstances. Coburg Lodge, Tulse Hill. A decent enough locality, doubtless; but —

'There's no harm in seeing her,' said Emmeline at length. 'Send a telegram, Clarence. Do you know, I think she may be the right kind of girl. I was thinking of someone awfully grand, and it's rather a relief. After all, you see, you — you are in business——'

'To be sure. And this girl seems to belong to a business family. I only wish she wrote in a more ladylike way.'

Emmeline set her house in order, filled the drawing–room with flowers, made the spare bedroom as inviting as possible, and, after luncheon, spent a good deal of time in adorning her person. She was a slight, pretty woman of something less than thirty; with a good, but pale, complexion, hair tending to auburn, sincere eyes. Her little vanities had no roots of ill–nature; she could admire without envy, and loved an orderly domestic life. Her husband's desire to increase his income had rather unsettled her; she exaggerated the importance of to–day's interview, and resolved with nervous energy to bring it to a successful issue, if Miss Derrick should prove a possible companion.

About four o'clock sounded the visitor's ring. From her bedroom window Emmeline had seen Miss Derrick's approach. As the distance from the station was only five minutes' walk, the stranger naturally came on foot. A dark girl, and of tolerably good features; rather dressy; with a carriage corresponding to the tone of her letter — an easy swing; head well up and shoulders squared. 'Oh, how I hope she isn't vulgar!' said Emmeline to herself. 'I don't like the bat — I don't. And that sunshade with the immense handle.' From the top of the stairs she heard a clear, unaffected voice: 'Mrs. Mumford at home?' Yes, the aspirate was sounded — thank goodness!

It surprised her, on entering the room, to find that Miss Derrick looked no less nervous than she was herself. The girl's cheeks were flushed, and she half choked over her 'How do you do?'

4

The Paying Guest

'I hope you had no difficulty in finding the house. I would have met you at the station if you had mentioned the train. Oh, but — how silly! — I shouldn't have known you.'

Miss Derrick laughed, and seemed of a sudden much more at ease.

'Oh, I like you for that!' she exclaimed mirthfully. 'It's just the kind of thing I say myself sometimes. And I'm so glad to see that you are — you mustn't be offended — I mean you're not the kind of person to be afraid of.'

They laughed together. Emmeline could not subdue her delight when she found that the girl really might be accepted as a lady. There were faults of costume undeniably; money had been misspent in several directions; but no glaring vulgarity hurt the eye. And her speech, though not strictly speaking refined, was free from the faults that betray low origin. Then, she seemed good–natured though there was something about her mouth not altogether charming.

'Do you know Sutton at all?' Emmeline inquired.

'Never was here before. But I like the look of it. I like this house, too. I suppose you know a lot of people here, Mrs. Mumford?'

'Well — no. There's only one family we know at all well. Our friends live in London. Of course they often come out here. I don't know whether you are acquainted with any of them. The Kirby Simpsons, of West Kensington; and Mrs. Hollings, of Highgate——'

Miss Derrick cast down her eyes and seemed to reflect. Then she spoke abruptly.

'I don't know any people to speak of. I ought to tell you that my mother has come down with me. She's waiting at the station till I go back; then she'll come and see you. You're surprised? Well, I had better tell you that I'm leaving home because I can't get on with my people. Mother and I have always quarrelled, but it has been worse than ever lately. I must explain that she has married a second time, and Mr. Higgins — I'm glad to say that isn't my name — has a daughter of his own by a first marriage; and we can't bear each other — Miss Higgins, I mean. Some day, if I come to live here, I daresay I shall tell you more. Mr. Higgins is rich, and I can't say he's unkind to me; he'll give me as much as I want; but I'm sure he'll be very glad to get me out of the house. I have no money of my own — worse luck! Well, we thought it best for me to come alone, first, and see — just to see, you know — whether we were likely to suit each other. Then mother will come and tell you all she has to say about me. Of course I know what it'll be. They all say I've a horrible temper. I don't think so myself; and I'm sure I don't think I should quarrel with you, you look so nice. But I can't get on at home, and it's better for all that we should part. I'm just two–and–twenty — do I look older? I haven't learnt to do anything, and I suppose I shall never need to.'

'Do you wish to see much society?' inquired Mrs. Mumford, who was thinking rapidly, 'or should you prefer a few really nice people? I'm afraid I don't quite understand yet whether you want society of the pleasure–seeking kind, or——'

She left the alternative vague. Miss Derrick again reflected for a moment before abruptly declaring herself.

'I feel sure that your friends are the kind I want to know. At all events, I should like to try. The great thing is to get away from home and see how things look.'

They laughed together. Emmeline, after a little more talk, offered to take her visitor over the house, and Miss Derrick had loud praise for everything she saw.

'What I like about you,' she exclaimed of a sudden, as they stood looking from a bedroom window on to the garden, 'is that you don't put on any — you know what I mean. People seem to me to be generally either low and ignorant, or so high and mighty there's no getting on with them at all. You're just what I wanted to find. Now I must go and send mother to see you.'

Emmeline protested against this awkward proceeding. Why should not both come together and have a cup of tea? If it were desired, Miss Derrick could step into the garden whilst her mother said whatever she wished to say. The girl assented, and in excellent spirits betook herself to the railway station. Emmeline waited something less than a quarter of an hour; then a hansom drove up, and Mrs. Higgins, after a deliberate survey of the house front, followed her daughter up the pathway.

The first sight of the portly lady made the situation clearer to Mrs. Mumford. Louise Derrick represented a certain stage of civilisation, a degree of conscious striving for better things; Mrs. Higgins was prosperous and self–satisfied vulgarity. Of a complexion much lighter than the girl's, she still possessed a coarse comeliness, which pointed back to the dairymaid type of damsel. Her features revealed at the same time a kindly nature and an irascible tendency. Monstrously overdressed, and weighted with costly gewgaws, she came forward panting and perspiring, and, before paying any heed to her hostess, closely surveyed the room.

'Mrs. Mumford,' said the girl, 'this is my mother. Mother, this is Mrs. Mumford. And now, please, let me go somewhere while you have your talk.'

'Yes, that'll be best, that'll be best,' exclaimed Mrs. Higgins. 'Dear, 'ow 'ot it is! Run out into the garden, Louise. Nice little 'ouse, Mrs. Mumford. And Louise seems quite taken with you. She doesn't take to people very easy, either. Of course, you can give satisfactory references? I like to do things in a business–like way. I understand your 'usband is in the City; shouldn't wonder if he knows some of Mr. 'Iggins's friends. Yes, I will take a cup, if you please. I've just had one at the station, but it's such thirsty weather. And what do you think of Louise? Because I'd very much rather you said plainly if you don't think you could get on.'

'But, indeed, I fancy we could, Mrs. Higgins.'

'Well, I'm sure I'm very glad of it. It isn't everybody can get on with Louise. I dessay she's told you a good deal about me and her stepfather. I don't think she's any reason to complain of the treatment——'

'She said you were both very kind to her,' interposed the hostess.

'I'm sure we try to be, and Mr. 'Iggins, he doesn't mind what he gives her. A five–pound note, if you'll believe me, is no more than a sixpence to him when he gives her presents. You see, Mrs. Rumford — no, Mumford, isn't it? — I was first married very young — scarcely eighteen, I was; and Mr. Derrick died on our wedding–day, two years after. Then came Mr. 'Iggins. Of course I waited a proper time. And one thing I can say, that no woman was ever 'appier with two 'usbands than I've been. I've two sons growing up, hearty boys as ever you saw. If it wasn't for this trouble with Louise——' She stopped to wipe her face. 'I dessay she's told you that Mr. 'Iggins, who was a widower when I met him, has a daughter of his first marriage — her poor mother died at the birth, and she's older than Louise. I don't mind telling you, Mrs. Mumford, she's close upon six–and–twenty, and nothing like so good–looking as Louise, neither. Mr. 'Iggins, he's kindness itself; but when it comes to differences between his daughter and my daughter, well, it isn't in nature he shouldn't favour his own. There's more be'ind, but I dessay you can guess, and I won't trouble you with things that don't concern you. And that's how it stands, you see.'

By a rapid calculation Emmeline discovered; with surprise, that Mrs. Higgins could not be much more than forty years of age. It must have been a life of gross self–indulgence that had made the woman look at least ten years older. This very undesirable parentage naturally affected Emmeline's opinion of Louise, whose faults began to show in a more pronounced light. One thing was clear: but for the fact that Louise aimed at a separation from her relatives, it would be barely possible to think of receiving her. If Mrs. Higgins thought of coming down to Sutton at unexpected moments — no, that was too dreadful.

'Should you wish, Mrs. Higgins, to entrust your daughter to me entirely?'

'My dear Mrs. Rumford, it's very little that my wishes has to do with it! She's made up her mind to leave 'ome, and all I can do is to see she gets with respectable people, which I feel sure you are; and of course I shall have your references.'

Emmeline turned pale at the suggestion. She all but decided that the matter must go no further.

'And what might your terms be — inclusive?' Mrs. Higgins proceeded to inquire.

At this moment a servant entered with tea, and Emmeline, sorely flurried, talked rapidly of the advantages of Sutton as a residence. She did not allow her visitor to put in a word till the door closed again. Then, with an air of decision, she announced her terms; they would be three guineas a week. It was half a guinea more than she and Clarence had decided to ask. She expected, she hoped, Mrs. Higgins would look grave. But nothing of the kind; Louise's mother seemed to think the suggestion very reasonable. Thereupon Emmeline added that, of course, the young lady would discharge her own laundress's bill. To this also Mrs. Higgins readily assented.

The Paying Guest

'A hundred and sixty pounds per annum!' Emmeline kept repeating to herself. And, alas! it looked as if she might have asked much more. The reference difficulty might be minimised by naming her own married sister, who lived at Blackheath, and Clarence's most intimate friend, Mr. Tarling, who held a good position in a City house, and had a most respectable address at West Kensington. But her heart misgave her. She dreaded her husband's return home.

The conversation was prolonged for half-an-hour. Emmeline gave her references, and in return requested the like from Mrs. Higgins. This astonished the good woman. Why, her husband was Messrs. 'Iggins of Fenchurch Street! Oh, a mere formality, Emmeline hastened to add — for Mr. Mumford's satisfaction. So Mrs. Higgins very pompously named two City firms, and negotiations, for the present, were at an end.

Louise, summoned to the drawing-room, looked rather tired of waiting.

'When can you have me, Mrs. Mumford?' she asked. 'I've quite made up my mind to come.'

'I'm afraid a day or two must pass, Miss Derrick——'

'The references, my dear,' began Mrs. Higgins.

'Oh, nonsense! It's all right; anyone can see.'

'There you go! Always cutting short the words in my mouth. I can't endure such behaviour, and I wonder what Mrs. Rumford thinks of it. I've given Mrs. Rumford fair warning——'

They wrangled for a few minutes, Emmeline feeling too depressed and anxious to interpose with polite commonplaces. When at length they took their leave, she saw the last of them with a sigh of thanksgiving. It had happened most fortunately that no one called this afternoon.

'Clarence, it's quite out of the question.' Thus she greeted her husband. 'The girl herself I could endure, but oh, her odious mother! — Three guineas a week! I could cry over the thought.'

The Paying Guest

By the first post in the morning came a letter from Louise. She wrote appealingly, touchingly. 'I know you couldn't stand my mother, but do please have me. I like Sutton, and I like your house, and I like you. I promise faithfully nobody from home shall ever come to see me, so don't be afraid. Of course if you won't have me, somebody else will; I've got two hundred to choose from, but I'd rather come to you. Do write and say I may come. I'm so sorry I quarrelled with mother before you. I promise never to quarrel with you. I'm very good–tempered when I get what I want.' With much more to the same effect.

'We will have her,' declared Mumford. 'Why not, if the old people keep away? — You are quite sure she sounds her h's?'

'Oh, quite. She has been to pretty good schools, I think. And I dare say I could persuade her to get other dresses and hats.'

'Of course you could. Really, it seems almost a duty to take her — doesn't it?'

So the matter was settled, and Mumford ran off gaily to catch his train.

Three days later Miss Derrick arrived, bringing with her something like half–a–ton of luggage. She bounded up the doorsteps, and, meeting Mrs. Mumford in the hall, kissed her fervently.

'I've got such heaps to tell you Mr. Higgins has given me twenty pounds to go on with — for myself; I mean; of course he'll pay everything else. How delighted I am to be here! Please pay the cabman I've got no change.'

A few hours before this there had come a letter from Mrs. Higgins; better written and spelt than would have seemed likely.

'Dear Mrs. Mumford,' it ran, 'L. is coming to–morrow morning, and I hope you won't repent. There's just one thing I meant to have said to you but forgot, so I'll say it now. If it should happen that any gentleman ot your acquaintance takes a fancy to L., and if it should come to anything, I'm sure both Mr. H. and me would be most thankful, and Mr. H. would behave handsome to her. And what's more, I'm sure he would be only too glad to show in a handsome way the thanks he would owe to you and Mr. M. — Very truly yours, Susan H. Higgins.'

CHAPTER II

'Runnymede' (so the Mumfords' house was named) stood on its own little plot of ground in one of the tree–shadowed roads which persuade the inhabitants of Sutton that they live in the country. It was of red brick, and double–fronted, with a porch of wood and stucco; bay windows on one side of the entrance, and flat on the other, made a contrast pleasing to the suburban eye. The little front garden had a close fence of unpainted lath, a characteristic of the neighbourhood. At the back of the house lay a long, narrow lawn, bordered with flower–beds, and shaded at the far end by a fine horse–chestnut.

Emmeline talked much of the delightful proximity of the Downs; one would have imagined her taking long walks over the breezy uplands to Ban stead or Epsom, or yet further afield The fact was, she saw no more of the country than if she had lived at Brixton. Her windows looked only upon the surrounding houses and their garden foliage. Occasionally she walked along the asphalte pavement of the Brighton Road — a nursemaids' promenade — as far as the stone which marks twelve miles from Westminster Bridge. Here, indeed, she breathed the air of the hills, but villas on either hand obstructed the view, and brought London much nearer than the measured distance. Like her friends and neighbours, Emmeline enjoyed Sutton because it was a most respectable little portion of the great town, set in a purer atmosphere. The country would have depressed her.

In this respect Miss Derrick proved a congenial companion. Louise made no pretence of rural inclinations, but had a great liking for tree–shadowed asphalte, for the results of elaborate horticulture, for the repose and the quiet of villadom.

'I should like to have a house just like this,' she declared, on her first evening at "Runnymede," talking with her host and hostess out in the garden. 'It's quite big enough, unless, of course, you have a very large family, which must be rather a bore.' She laughed ingenuously. 'And one gets to town so easily. What do you pay for your season–ticket, Mr. Mumford? Oh, well! that isn't much. I almost think I shall get one.'

'Do you wish to go up very often, then?' asked Emmeline, reflecting on her new responsibilities.

'Oh! not every day, of course. But a season–ticket saves the bother each time, and you have a sort of feeling, you know, that you can be in town whenever you like.'

It had not hitherto been the Mumfords' wont to dress for dinner, but this evening they did so, and obviously to Miss Derrick's gratification. She herself appeared in a dress which altogether outshone that of her hostess. Afterwards, in private, she drew Emmeline's attention to this garb, and frankly asked her opinion of it.

'Very nice indeed,' murmured the married lady, with a good–natured smile. 'Perhaps a little——'

'There, I know what you're going to say. You think it's too showy. Now I want you to tell me just what you think about everything — everything. I shan't be offended. I'm not so silly. You know I've come here to learn all sorts of things. To–morrow you shall go over all my dresses with me, and those you don't like I'll get rid of. I've never had anyone to tell me what's nice and what isn't. I want to be — oh, well, you know what I mean.'

'But, my dear,' said Emmeline, 'there's something I don't quite understand. You say I'm to speak plainly, and so I will. How is it that you haven't made friends long ago with the sort of people you wish to know? It isn't as if you were in poor circumstances.'

'How could I make friends with nice people when I was ashamed to have them at home? The best I know are quite poor — girls I went to school with. They're much better educated than I am, but they make their own living, and so I can't see very much of them, and I'm not sure they want to see much of me. I wish I knew what people think of me; they call me vulgar, I believe — the kind I'm speaking of. Now, do tell me, Mrs. Mumford, am I vulgar?'

'My dear Miss Derrick—' Emmeline began in protest, but was at once interrupted.

'Oh! that isn't what I want. You must call me Louise, or Lou, if you like, and just say what you really think. Yes, I see, I am rather vulgar, and what can you expect? Look at mother; and if you saw Mr. Higgins, oh! The mistake I made was to leave school so soon. I got sick of it, and left at sixteen, and of course the idiots at home — I mean the foolish people — let me have my own way. I'm not clever, you know, and I didn't get on well at school. They used to say I could do much better if I liked, and perhaps it was more laziness than stupidity, though I don't care for books — I wish I did. I've had lots of friends, but I never keep them for very long. I don't know whether it's their fault or mine. My oldest friends are Amy Barker and Muriel Featherstone; they were both at the school at Clapham, and now Amy does type–writing in the City, and Muriel is at a photographer's. They're awfully nice girls, and t like them so much; but then, you see, they haven't enough money to live in what I call a nice way, and, you know, I should never think of asking them to advise me about my dresses, or anything of that kind. A friend of mine once began to say something and I didn't like it; after that we had nothing to do with each other.'

Emmeline could not hide her amusement.

'Well, that's just it,' went on the other frankly. 'I have rather a sharp temper, and I suppose I don't get on well with most people. I used to quarrel dreadfully with some of the girls at school — the uppish sort. And yet all the time I wanted to be friends with them. But, of course, I could never have taken them home.'

Mrs. Mumford began to read the girl's character, and to understand how its complexity had shaped her life. She was still uneasy as to the impression this guest would make upon their friends, but on the whole it seemed probable that Louise would conscientiously submit herself to instruction, and do her very best to be "nice." Clarence's opinion was still favourable; he pronounced Miss Derrick "very amusing," and less of a savage than his wife's description had led him to expect.

Having the assistance of two servants and a nurse–girl, Emmeline was not overburdened with domestic work. She soon found it fortunate that her child, a girl of two years old, needed no great share of her attention; for Miss Derrick, though at first she affected an extravagant interest in the baby, very soon had enough of that plaything, and showed a decided preference for Emmeline's society out of sight and hearing of nursery affairs. On the afternoon of the second day they went together to call upon Mrs. Fentiman, who lived at a distance of a quarter of an hour's walk, in a house called "Hazeldene"; a semi–detached house, considerably smaller than "Runnymede," and neither without nor within so pleasant to look upon. Mrs. Fentiman, a tall, hard–featured, but amiable lady, had two young children who occupied most of her time; at present one of them was ailing, and the mother could talk of nothing else but this distressing circumstance. The call lasted only for ten minutes, and Emmeline felt that her companion was disappointed.

'Children are a great trouble,' Louise remarked, when they had left the house. 'People ought never to marry unless they can keep a lot of servants. Not long ago I was rather fond of somebody, but I wouldn't have him because he had no money. Don't you think I was quite right?'

'I have no doubt you were.'

'And now,' pursued the girl, poking the ground with her sunshade as she walked, 'there's somebody else. And that's one of the things I want to tell you about. He has about three hundred a year. It isn't much, of course; but I suppose Mr. Higgins would give me something. And yet I'm sure it won't come to anything. Let's go home and have a good talk, shall we?'

Mrs. Higgins's letter had caused Emmeline and her husband no little amusement; but at the same time it led them to reflect. Certainly they numbered among their acquaintances one or two marriageable young men who might perchance be attracted by Miss Derrick, especially if they learnt that Mr. Higgins was disposed to 'behave handsomely' to his stepdaughter; but the Mumfords had no desire to see Louise speedily married. To the bribe with which the letter ended they could give no serious thought. Having secured their "paying guest," they hoped she would remain with them for a year or two at least. But already Louise had dropped hints such as Emmeline could not fail to understand, and her avowal of serious interest in a lover came rather as an annoyance than a surprise to Mrs. Mumford.

It was a hot afternoon, and they had tea brought out into the garden, under the rustling leaves of the chestnut.

'You don't know anyone else at Sutton except Mrs. Fentiman?' said Louise, as she leaned back in the wicker chair.

'Not intimately. But some of our friends from London will be coming on Sunday. I've asked four people to lunch.'

The Paying Guest

'How jolly! Of course you'll tell me all about them before then. But I want to talk about Mr. Cobb. Please, two lumps of sugar. I've known him for about a year and a half. We seem quite old friends, and he writes to me; I don't answer the letters, unless there's something to say. To tell the truth, I don't like him.'

'How can that be if you seem old friends?'

'Well, he likes me; and there's no harm in that, so long as he understands. I'm sure you wouldn't like him. He's a rough, coarse sort of man, and has a dreadful temper.'

'Good gracious! What is his position?'

'Oh, he's connected with the what–d'ye–call–it Electric Lighting Company. He travels about a good deal. I shouldn't mind that; it must be rather nice not to have one's husband always at home. Just now I believe he's in Ireland. I shall be having a letter from him very soon, no doubt. He doesn't know I've left home, and it'll make him wild. Yes, that's the kind of man he is. Fearfully jealous, and such a temper! If I married him, I'm quite sure he would beat me some day.'

'Oh!' Emmeline exclaimed. 'How can you have anything to do with such a man?'

'He's very nice sometimes,' answered Louise, thoughtfully.

'But do you really mean that he is "rough and coarse"?'

'Yes, I do. You couldn't call him a gentleman. I've never seen his people; they live somewhere a long way off; and I shouldn't wonder if they are a horrid lot. His last letter was quite insulting. He said — let me see, what was it? Yes — "You have neither heart nor brains, and 1 shall do my best not to waste another thought on you?" What do you think of that?'

'It seems very extraordinary, my dear. How can he write to you in that way if you never gave him any encouragement?'

'Well, but I suppose I have done. We've met on the Common now and then, and — and that kind of thing. I'm afraid you're shocked, Mrs. Mumford. I know it isn't the way that nice people behave, and I'm going to give it up.'

'Does your mother know him?'

'Oh, yes! there's no secret about it. Mother rather likes him. Of course he behaves himself when he's at the house. I've a good mind to ask him to call here so that you could see him. Yes, I should like you to sea him. You wouldn't mind?'

'Not if you really wish it, Louise. But — I can't help thinking you exaggerate his faults.'

'Not a bit. He's a regular brute when he gets angry.'

'My dear,' Emmeline interposed softly, 'that isn't quite a ladylike expression.'

'No, it isn't. Thank you, Mrs. Mumford. I meant to say he is horrid — very disagreeable. Then there s something else I want to tell you about. Cissy Higgins — that's Mr. Higgins's daughter, you know — is half engaged to a man called Bowling — an awful idiot——'

'I don't think I would use that word, dear.'

'Thank you, Mrs. Mumford. I mean to say he's a regular silly. But he's in a very good position — a partner in Jannaway Brothers of Woolwich, though he isn't thirty yet. Well, now, what do you think? Mr. Bowling doesn't seem to know his own mind, and just lately he's been paying so much attention to me that Cissy has got quite frantic about it. This was really and truly the reason why I left home.'

'I see,' murmured the listener, with a look of genuine interest.

'Yes. They wanted to get me out of the way. There wasn't the slightest fear that I should try to cut Cissy Higgins out; but it was getting very awkward for her, I admit. Now that's the kind of thing that doesn't go on among nice people, isn't it?'

'But what do you mean, Louise, when you say that Miss Higgins and Mr. — Mr. Bowling are half engaged?'

The Paying Guest

'Oh, I mean she has refused him once, just for form's sake; but he knows very well she means to have him. People of your kind don't do that sort of thing, do they?'

'I hardly know,' Emmeline replied, colouring a little at certain private reminiscences. 'And am I to understand that you wouldn't on any account listen to Mr. Bowling?'

Louise laughed.

'Oh, there's no knowing what I might do to spite Cissy. We hate each other, of course. But I can't fancy myself marrying him, He has a long nose, and talks through it. And he says "think you" for "thank you," and he sings — oh, to hear him sing! I can't bear the man.'

The matter of this conversation Emmeline reported to her husband at night, and they agreed in the hope that neither Mr. Cobb nor Mr. Bowling would make an appearance at "Runnymede." Mumford opined that these individuals were "cads." Small wonder, he said, that the girl wished to enter a new social sphere. His wife, on the other hand, had a suspicion that Miss Derrick would not be content to see the last of Mr. Cobb. He, the electrical engineer, or whatever he was, could hardly be such a ruffian as the girl depicted. His words, 'You have neither heart nor brains,' seemed to indicate anything but a coarse mind.

'But what a bad—tempered lot they are!' Mumford observed. 'I suppose people of that sort quarrel and abuse each other merely to pass the time. They seem to be just one degree above the roughs who come to blows and get into the police court. You must really do your best to get the girl out of it; I'm sure she is worthy of better things.'

'She is — in one way,' answered his wife judicially. 'But her education stopped too soon. I doubt if it's possible to change her very much. And — I really should like, after all, to see Mr. Cobb.'

Mumford broke into a laugh.

'There you go! The eternal feminine. You'll have her married in six months.'

'Don't be vulgar, Clarence. And we've talked enough of Louise for the present.'

17

Miss Derrick's presentiment that a letter from Mr. Cobb would soon reach her was justified the next day; it arrived in the afternoon, readdressed from Tulse Hill. Emmeline observed the eagerness with which this epistle was pounced upon and carried off for private perusal. She saw, too, that in half–an–hour's time Louise left the house — doubtless to post a reply. But, to her surprise, not a word of the matter escaped Miss Derrick during the whole evening.

In her school–days, Louise had learned to "play the piano," but, caring little or nothing for music, she had hardly touched a key for several years. Now the idea possessed her that she must resume her practising, and to–day she had spent hours at the piano, with painful effect upon Mrs. Mumford's nerves. After dinner she offered to play to Mumford, and he, good–natured fellow, stood by her to turn over the leaves. Emmeline, with fancy work in her hands, watched the two. She was not one of the most foolish of her sex, but it relieved her when Clarence moved away.

The next morning Louise was an hour late for breakfast. She came down when Mumford had left the house, and Emmeline saw with surprise that she was dressed for going out.

'Just a cup of coffee, please. I've no appetite this morning, and I want to catch a train for Victoria as soon as possible.'

'When will you be back?'

'Oh, I don't quite know. To tea, I think.'

The girl had all at once grown reticent, and her lips showed the less amiable possibilities of their contour.

CHAPTER III

At dinner–time she had not returned. It being Saturday, Mumford was back early in the afternoon, and Miss Derrick's absence caused no grief. Emmeline could play with baby in the garden, whilst her husband smoked his pipe and looked on in the old comfortable way. They already felt that domestic life was not quite the same with a stranger to share it. Doubtless they would get used to the new restraints; but Miss Derrick must not expect them to disorganise their mealtimes on her account. Promptly at half—past seven they sat down to dine, and had just risen from the table, when Louise appeared.

She was in excellent spirits, without a trace of the morning's ill—humour. No apologies! If she didn't feel quite free to come and go, without putting people out, there would be no comfort in life. A slice of the joint, that was all she wanted, and she would have done in a few minutes.

'I've taken tickets for Toole's Theatre on Monday night. You must both come. You can, can't you?'

Mumford and his wife glanced at each other. Yes, they could go; it was very kind of Miss Derrick; but——

'That's all right, it'll be jolly. The idea struck me in the train, as I was going up; so I took a cab from Victoria and booked the places first thing. Third row from the front, dress circle; the best I could do. Please let me have my dinner alone. Mrs. Mumford, I want to tell you something afterwards.'

Clarence went round to see his friend Fentiman, with whom he usually had a chat on Saturday evening. Emmeline was soon joined by the guest in the drawing—room.

'There, you may read that,' said Louise, holding out a letter. 'It's from Mr. Cobb; came yesterday, but I didn't care to talk about it then. Yes, please read it; I want you to.'

Reluctantly, but with curiosity, Emmeline glanced over the sheet. Mr. Cobb wrote in ignorance of Miss Derrick's having left home. It was a plain, formal letter, giving a brief account of his doings in Ireland, and making a request that Louise would meet him, if possible, on Streatham Common, at three o'clock on Saturday afternoon. And he signed himself—— 'Very sincerely yours.'

'I made up my mind at once,' said the girl, 'that I wouldn't meet him. That kind of thing will have to stop. I'm not going to think any more of him, and it's better to make him understand it at once — isn't it?'

Emmeline heartily concurred.

'Still,' pursued the other, with an air of great satisfaction, 'I thought I had better go home for this afternoon. Because when he didn't see me on the Common he was pretty sure to call at the house, and I didn't want mother or Cissy to be talking about me to him before he had heard my own explanation.'

'Didn't you answer the letter?' asked Emmeline.

'No. I just sent a line to mother, to let her know I was coming over to–day, so that she might stay at home. Well, and it happened just as I thought. Mr. Cobb came to the house at half–past three. But before that I'd had a terrible row with Cissy. That isn't a nice expression, I know, but it really was one of our worst quarrels. Mr. Bowling hasn't been near since I left, and Cissy is furious. She said such things that I had to tell her very plainly what I thought of her; and she positively foamed at the mouth! "Now look here," she said, "if I find out that he goes to Sutton, you'll see what will happen." "What will happen?" I asked. "Father will stop your allowance, and you'll have to get on as best you can." "Oh, very well," I said, "in that case I shall marry Mr. Bowling." You should have seen her rage! "You said you wouldn't marry him if he had ten thousand a year!" she screamed. "I dare say I did; but if I've nothing to live upon——" "You can marry your Mr. Cobb, can't you?" And she almost cried; and I should have felt sorry for her if she hadn't made me so angry. "No," I said, "I can't marry Mr. Cobb. And I never dreamt of marrying Mr. Cobb. And——"'

Emmeline interposed.

'Really, Louise, that kind of talk isn't at all ladylike. What a pity you went home.'

'Yes, I was sorry for it afterwards. I shan't go again for a long time; I promise you I won't. However, Mr. Cobb came, and I saw him alone. He was astonished when he heard what had been going on; he was astonished at me, too — I mean, the way I spoke. I wanted him to understand at once that there was nothing between us; I talked in rather a — you know the sort of way.' She raised her chin slightly, and looked down from under her eyelids. 'Oh, I assure you I behaved quite nicely. But he got into a rage, as he always does, and began to call me names, and I wouldn't stand it. "Mr. Cobb," I said, very severely, "either you will conduct yourself properly, or you will leave the house." Then he tried another tone, and said very different things — the kind of thing one likes to hear, you know; but I pretended that I didn't care for it a bit. "It's all over between us then?" he shouted at last; yes, really shouted, and I'm sure people must have heard. "All over?" I said. "But there never was anything — nothing serious." "Oh, all right. Good–bye, then." And off he rushed. And I dare say I've seen the last of him — for a time.'

'Now do try to live quietly, my dear,' said Emmeline. 'Go on with your music, and read a little each day——'

'Yes, that's just what I'm going to do, dear Mrs. Mumford. And your friends will be here to–morrow; it'll be so quiet and nice. And on Monday we shall go to the theatre, just for a change. And I'm not going to think of those people. It's all settled. I shall live very quietly indeed.'

She banged on the piano till nearly eleven o'clock, and went off to bed with a smile of virtuous contentment.

The guests who arrived on Sunday morning were Mr. and Mrs. Grove, Mr. Bilton, and Mr. Dunnill. Mrs. Grove was Emmeline's elder sister, a merry, talkative, kindly woman. Aware of the circumstances, she at once made friends with Miss Derrick, and greatly pleased that young lady by a skilful blending of "superior" talk with easy homeliness. Mr. Bilton, a stockbroker's clerk, represented the better kind of City young man — athletic, yet intelligent, spirited without vulgarity a breezy, good–humoured, wholesome fellow. He came down on his bicycle, and would return in the same way. Louise at once made a resolve to learn cycling.

'I wish you lived at Sutton, Mr. Bilton. I should ask you to teach me.'

'I'm really very sorry that I don't,' replied the young man discreetly.

'Oh, never mind. I'll find somebody.'

The fourth arrival, Mr. Dunnill, was older and less affable. He talked chiefly with Mr. Grove, a very quiet, somewhat careworn man; neither of them seemed able to shake off business, but they did not obtrude it on the company in general. The day passed pleasantly, but in Miss Derrick's opinion, rather soberly. Doing her best to fascinate Mr. Bilton, she felt a slight disappointment at her inability to engross his attention, and at the civil friendliness which he thought a sufficient reply to her gay sallies. For so good–looking and well–dressed a man he struck her as singularly reserved. But perhaps he was "engaged"; yes, that must be the explanation. When the guests had left, she put a plain question to Mrs. Mumford.

'I don't think he is engaged,' answered Emmeline, who on the whole was satisfied with Miss Derrick's demeanour throughout the day.

'Oh! But, of course, he may be, without you knowing it. Or is it always made known?'

'There's no rule about it, my dear.'

'Well, they're very nice people,' said Louise, with a little sigh. 'And I like your sister so much. I'm glad she asked me to go and see her. Is Mr. Bilton often at her house? — Don't misunderstand me, Mrs. Mumford. It's only that I do like men's society; there's no harm, is there? And people like Mr. Bilton are very different from those I've known; and I want to see more of them, you know.'

'There's no harm in saying that to me, Louise,' replied Mrs. Mumford. 'But pray be careful not to seem "forward." People think — and say — such disagreeable things.'

Miss Derrick was grateful, and again gave an assurance that repose and modesty should be the rule of her life.

At the theatre on Monday evening she exhibited a childlike enjoyment which her companions could not but envy. The freshness of her sensibilities was indeed remarkable, and Emmeline observed with pleasure that her mind seemed to have a very wholesome tone. Louise might commit follies, and be guilty of bad taste to any extent, but nothing in her savoured of depravity.

Tuesday she spent at home, pretending to read a little, and obviously thinking a great deal. On Wednesday morning she proposed of a sudden that Emmeline should go up to town with her on a shopping expedition. They had already turned over her wardrobe, numerous articles whereof were condemned by Mrs. Mumford's taste, and by Louise cheerfully sacrificed; she could not rest till new purchases had been made. So, after early luncheon, they took train to Victoria, Louise insisting that all the expenses should be hers. By five o'clock she had laid out some fifteen pounds, vastly to her satisfaction. They took tea at a restaurant, and reached Sutton not long before Mumford's return.

On Friday they went to London again, to call upon Mrs. Grove. Louise promised that this should be her last "outing" for a whole week. She admitted a feeling of restlessness, but after to–day she would overcome it. And that night she apologised formally to Mumford for taking his wife so much from home.

'Please don't think I shall always be running about like this. I feel that I'm settling down. We are going to be very comfortable and quiet.'

And, to the surprise of her friends, more than a week went by before she declared that a day in town was absolutely necessary. Mr. Higgins had sent her a fresh supply of money, as there were still a few things she needed to purchase. But this time Emmeline begged her to go alone, and Louise seemed quite satisfied with the arrangement.

Early in the afternoon, as Mrs. Mumford was making ready to go out, the servant announced to her that a gentleman had called to see Miss Derrick; on learning that Miss Derrick was away, he had asked sundry questions, and ended by requesting an interview with Mrs. Mumford. His name was Cobb.

'Show him into the drawing–room,' said Emmeline, a trifle agitated. 'I will be down in a few moments.'

Beset by anxious anticipations, she entered the room, and saw before her a figure not wholly unlike what she had imagined: a wiry, resolute–looking man, with knitted brows, lips close–set, and heavy feet firmly planted on the carpet. He was respectably dressed, but nothing more, and in his large bare hands held a brown hat marked with a grease spot. One would have judged him a skilled mechanic. When he began to speak, his blunt but civil phrases were in keeping with this impression. He had not the tone of an educated man, yet committed no vulgar errors.

'My name is Cobb. I must beg your pardon for troubling you. Perhaps you have heard of me from Miss Derrick?'

'Yes, Mr. Cobb, your name has been mentioned,' Emmeline replied nervously. 'Will you sit down?'

The Paying Guest

'Thank you, I will.'

He twisted his hat about, and seemed to prepare with difficulty the next remark, which at length burst, rather than fell, from his lips.

'I wanted to see Miss Derrick. I suppose she is still living with you? They told me so.'

A terrible man, thought Emmeline, when roused to anger; his words must descend like sledge—hammers. And it would not take much to anger him. For all that, he had by no means a truculent countenance. He was trying to smile, and his features softened agreeably enough. The more closely she observed him, the less grew Emmeline's wonder that Louise felt an interest in the man.

'Miss Derrick is likely to stay with us for some time, I believe. She has only gone to town, to do some shopping.'

'I see. When I met her last she talked a good deal about you, Mrs. Mumford, and that's why I thought I would ask to see you. You have a good deal of influence over her.'

'Do you think so?' returned Emmeline, not displeased. 'I hope I may use it for her good.'

'So do I. But — well, it comes to this, Mrs. Mumford. She seemed to hint — though she didn't exactly say so — that you were advising her to have nothing more to do with me. Of course you don't know me, and I've no doubt you do what you think the best for her. I should feel it a kindness if you would just tell me whether you are really persuading her to think no more about me.'

It was an alarming challenge. Emmeline's fears returned; she half expected an outbreak of violence. The man was growing very nervous, and his muscles showed the working of strong emotion.

'I have given her no such advice, Mr. Cobb,' she answered, with an attempt at calm dignity. 'Miss Derrick's private affairs don't at all concern me. In such matters as this she is really quite old enough to judge for herself.'

24

The Paying Guest

'That's what I should have said,' remarked Mr. Cobb sturdily. 'I hope you'll excuse me; I don't wish to make myself offensive. After what she said to me when we met last, I suppose most men would just let her go her own way. But — but somehow I can't do that. The thing is, I can't trust what she says; I don't believe she knows her own mind. And so long as you tell me that you're not interfering — I mean, that you don't think it right to set her against me——'

'I assure you, nothing of the kind.'

There was a brief silence, then Cobb's voice again sounded with blunt emphasis.

'We're neither of us very good–tempered. We've known each other about a year, and we must have quarrelled about fifty times.'

'Do you think, then,' ventured the hostess, 'that it would ever be possible for you to live peacefully together?'

'Yes, I do,' was the robust answer. 'It would be a fight for the upper hand, but I know who'd get it, and after that things would be all right.'

Emmeline could not restrain a laugh, and her visitor joined in it with a heartiness which spoke in his favour.

'I promise you, Mr. Cobb, that I will do nothing whatever against your interests.'

'That's very kind of you, and it's all I wanted to know.'

He stood up. Emmeline, still doubtful how to behave, asked him if he would call on another day, when Miss Derrick might be at home.

'It's only by chance I was able to get here this afternoon,' he replied. 'I haven't much time to go running about after her, and that's where I'm at a disadvantage. I don't know whether there's anyone else, and I'm not asking you to tell me, if you know. Of course I have to take my chance; but so long as you don't speak against me — and she thinks a great deal of your advice——'

'I'm very glad to be assured of that. All I shall do, Mr. Cobb, is to keep before her mind the duty of behaving straightforwardly.'

'That's the thing! Nobody can ask more than that.'

Emmeline hesitated, but could not dismiss him without shaking hands. That he did not offer to do so until invited, though he betrayed no sense of social inferiority, seemed another point in his favour.

CHAPTER IV

Not half an hour after Cobb's departure Louise returned. Emmeline was surprised to see her back so soon; they met near the railway station as Mrs. Mumford was on her way to a shop in High Street.

'Isn't it good of me! If I had stayed longer I should have gone home to quarrel with Cissy; but I struggled against the temptation. Going to the grocer's? Oh, do let me go with you, and see how you do that kind of thing. I never gave an order at the grocer's in my life — no, indeed I never did. Mother and Cissy have always looked after that. And I want to learn about housekeeping; you promised to teach me.'

Emmeline made no mention of Mr. Cobb's call until they reached the house.

'He came here!' Louise exclaimed, reddening. 'What impudence! I shall at once write and tell him that his behaviour is outrageous. Am I to be hunted like this?'

Her wrath seemed genuine enough; but she was vehemently eager to learn all that had passed. Emmeline made a truthful report.

'You're quite sure that was all? Oh, his impertinence! Well, and now that you've seen him, don't you understand how — how impossible it is?'

'I shall say nothing more about it, Louise. It isn't my business to——'

The girl's face threatened a tempest. As Emmeline was moving away, she rudely obstructed her.

'I insist on you telling me what you think. It was abominable of him to come when I wasn't at home; and I don't think you ought to have seen him. You've no right to keep your thoughts to yourself!'

Mrs. Mumford was offended, and showed it.

'I have a perfect right, and I shall do so. Please don't let us quarrel. You may be fond of it, but I am not.'

Louise went from the room and remained invisible till just before dinner, when she came down with a grave and rather haughty countenance. To Mumford's remarks she replied with curt formality; he, prepared for this state of things, began conversing cheerfully with his wife, and Miss Derrick kept silence. After dinner, she passed out into the garden.

'It won't do,' said Mumford. 'The house is upset. I'm afraid we shall have to get rid of her.'

'If she can't behave herself, I'm afraid we must. It's my fault. I ought to have known that it would never do.'

At half-past ten, Louise was still sitting out of doors in the dark. Emmeline, wishing to lock up for the night, went to summon her troublesome guest.

'Hadn't you better come in?'

'Yes. But I think you are very unkind, Mrs. Mumford.'

'Miss Derrick, I really can't do anything but leave you alone when you are in such an unpleasant hum our.'

'But that's just what you oughtn't to do. When I'm left alone I sulk, and that's bad for all of us. If you would just get angry and give me what I deserve, it would be all over very soon.'

'You are always talking about "nice" people. Nice people don't have scenes of that kind.'

'No, I suppose not. And I'm very sorry, and if you'll let me beg your pardon——. There, and we might have made it up hours ago. I won't ask you to tell me what you think of Mr. Cobb. I've written him the kind of letter his impudence deserves.'

'Very well. We won't talk of it any more. And if you could be a little quieter in your manners, Louise——'

'I will, I promise I will I Let me say good–night to Mr. Mumford.'

For a day or two there was halcyon weather. On Saturday afternoon Louise hired a carriage and took her friends for a drive into the country; at her special request the child accompanied them. Nothing could have been more delightful. She had quite made up her mind to have a house, some day, at Sutton. She hoped the Mumfords would "always" live there, that they might perpetually enjoy each other's society. What were the rents? she inquired. Well, to begin with, she would be content with one of the smaller houses; a modest, semidetached little place, like those at the far end of Cedar Road. They were perfectly respectable — were they not? How this change in her station was to come about Louise offered no hint, and did not seem to think of the matter.

Then restlessness again came upon her. One day she all but declared her disappointment that the Mumfords saw so few people. Emmeline, repeating this to her husband, avowed a certain compunction.

'I almost feel that I deliberately misled her. You know, Clarence, in our first conversation I mentioned the Kirby Simpsons and Mrs. Hollings, and I feel sure she remembers. It wouldn't be nice to be taking her money on false pretences, would it?'

'Oh, don't trouble. It's quite certain she has someone in mind whom she means to marry before long.'

'I can't help thinking that. But I don't know who it can be. She had a letter this morning in a man's writing, and didn't speak of it. It wasn't Mr. Cobb.'

Louise, next day, put a point–blank question.

'Didn't you say that you knew some people at West Kensington?'

The Paying Guest

'Oh, yes,' answered Emmeline, carelessly. 'The Kirby Simpsons. They're away from home.'

'I'm sorry for that. Isn't there anyone else we could go and see, or ask over here?'

'I think it very likely Mr. Bilton will come down in a few days.'

Louise received Mr. Bilton's name with moderate interest. But she dropped the subject, and seemed to reconcile herself to domestic pleasures.

It was on the evening of this day that Emmeline received a letter which gave her much annoyance. Her sister, Mrs. Grove, wrote thus:

'How news does get about! And what ridiculous forms it takes! Here is Mrs. Powell writing to me from Birmingham, and she says she has heard that you have taken in the daughter of some wealthy parvenu, for a consideration, to train her in the ways of decent society! Just the kind of thing Mrs. Powell would delight in talking about — she is so very malicious. Where she got her information I can't imagine. She doesn't give the slightest hint. "They tell me" — I copy her words — "that the girl is all but a savage, and does and says the most awful things. I quite admire Mrs. Mumford's courage. I've heard of people doing this kind of thing, and I always wondered how they got on with their friends." Of course I have written to contradict this rubbish. But it's very annoying, I'm sure.'

Mumford was angry. The source of these fables must be either Bilton or Dunnill, yet he had not thought either of them the kind of men to make mischief. Who else knew anything of the affair? Searching her memory, Emmeline recalled a person unknown to her, a married lady, who had dropped in at Mrs. Grove's when she and Louise were there.

'I didn't like her — a supercilious sort of person. And she talked a great deal of her acquaintance with important people. It's far more likely to have come from her than from either of those men. I shall write and tell Molly so.'

They began to feel uncomfortable, and seriously thought of getting rid of the burden so imprudently undertaken. Louise, the next day, wanted to take Emmeline to town, and showed dissatisfaction when she had to go unaccompanied. She stayed till late in the evening, and came back with a gay account of her calls upon two or three old friends — the girls of whom she had spoken to Mrs. Mumford. One of them, Miss Featherstone, she had taken to dine with her at a restaurant, and afterwards they had spent an hour or two at Miss Featherstone's lodgings.

'I didn't go near Tulse Hill, and if you knew how I am wondering what is going on there! Not a line from anyone. I shall write to mother to−morrow.'

Emmeline produced a letter which had arrived for Miss Derrick.

'Why didn't you give it me before?' Louise exclaimed, impatiently.

'My dear, you had so much to tell me. I waited for the first pause.'

'That isn't from home,' said the girl, after a glance at the envelope. 'It's nothing.'

After saying good−night, she called to Emmeline from her bedroom door. Entering the room, Mrs. Mumford saw the open letter in Louise's hand, and read in her face a desire of confession.

'I want to tell you something. Don't be in a hurry; just a few minutes. This letter is from Mr. Bowling. Yes, and I've had one from him before, and I was obliged to answer it.'

'Do you mean they are love−letters?'

'Yes, I'm afraid they are. And it's so stupid, and I'm so vexed. I don't want to have anything to do with him, as I told you long ago.' Louise often used expressions which to a stranger would have implied that her intimacy with Mrs. Mumford was of years' standing. 'He wrote for the first time last week. Such a silly letter! I wish you would read it. Well, he said that it was all over between him and Cissy, and that he cared only for me, and always had, and always would — you know how men write. He said he considered himself quite free. Cissy had refused him, and wasn't that enough? Now that I was away from home, he could write to me, and wouldn't I let him see me? Of course I wrote that I didn't want to see him, and I thought he was behaving very badly — though I don't really think so, because it's all that idiot Cissy's fault. Didn't I do quite right?'

The Paying Guest

'I think so.'

'Very well. And now he's writing again, you see; oh, such a lot of rubbish! I can hear him saying it all through his nose. Do tell me what I ought to do next.'

'You must either pay no attention to the letter, or reply so that he can't possibly misunderstand you.'

'Call him names, you mean?'

'My dear Louise!'

'But that's the only way with such men. I suppose you never were bothered with them. I think I'd better not write at all.'

Emmeline approved this course, and soon left Miss Derrick to her reflections.

The next day Louise carried out her resolve to write for information regarding the progress of things at Coburg Lodge. She had not long to wait for a reply, and it was of so startling a nature that she ran at once to Mrs. Mumford, whom she found in the nursery.

'Do please come down. Here's something I must tell you about. What do you think mother says? I've to go back home again at once.'

'What's the reason?' Emmeline inquired, knowing not whether to be glad or sorry.

'I'll read it to you: — "Dear Lou," she says, "you've made a great deal of trouble, and I hope you're satisfied. Things are all upside down, and I've never seen dada" — that's Mr. Higgins, of course — "I've never seen dada in such a bad temper, not since first I knew him. Mr. B." — that's Mr. Bowling, you know — "has told him plain that he doesn't think any more of Cissy, and that nothing mustn't be expected of him." — Oh what sweet letters mother does write! — "That was when dada went and asked him about his intentions, as he couldn't help doing, because Cissy is fretting so. It's all over, and of course you're the cause of it; and, though I can't blame you as much as the others do, I think you are to blame. And Cissy said she must go to the seaside to get over it, and she went off yesterday to Margate to your Aunt Annie's boarding–house, and there she says she shall stay as long as she doesn't feel quite well, and dada has to pay two guineas a week for her. So he says at once, 'Now Loo 'll have to come back. I'm not going to pay for the both of them boarding out,' he says. And he means it. He has told me to write to you at once, and you're to come as soon as you can, and he won't be responsible to Mrs. Mumford for more than another week's payment." — There! But I shan't go, for all that. The idea! I left home just to please them, and now I'm to go back just when it suits their convenience. Certainly not.'

'But what will you do, Louise,' asked Mrs. Mumford, 'if Mr. Higgins is quite determined?'

'Do? Oh! I shall settle it easy enough. I shall write at once to the old man and tell him I'm getting on so nicely in every way that I couldn't dream of leaving you. It's all nonsense, you'll see.'

Emmeline and her husband held a council that night, and resolved that, whatever the issue of Louise's appeal to her stepfather, this was a very good opportunity for getting rid of their guest. They would wait till Louise made known the upshot of her negotiations. It seemed probable that Mr. Higgins would spare them the unpleasantness of telling Miss Derrick she must leave. If not, that disagreeable necessity must be faced.

'I had rather cut down expenses all round,' said Emmeline, 'than have our home upset in this way. It isn't like home at all. Louise is a whirlwind, and the longer she stays, the worse it'll be.'

'Yes, it won't do at all,' Mumford assented. 'By the bye, I met Bilton to–day, and he asked after Miss Derrick. I didn't like his look or his tone at all. I feel quite sure there's a joke going round at our expense. Confound it!'

'Never mind. It'll be over in a day or two, and it'll be a lesson to you, Clarence, won't it?'

'I quite admit that the idea was mine,' her husband replied, rather irritably. 'But it wasn't I who accepted the girl as a suitable person.'

'And certainly it wasn't me!' rejoined Emmeline. 'You will please to remember that I said again and again——'

The Paying Guest

'Oh, hang it, Emmy! We made a blunder, both of us, and don't let us make it worse by wrangling about it. There you are; people of that class bring infection into the house. If she stayed here a twelvemonth, we should have got to throwing things at each other.'

The answer to Louise's letter of remonstrance came in the form of Mrs. Higgins herself Shortly before luncheon that lady drove up to "Runnymede" in a cab, and her daughter, who had just returned from a walk, was startled to hear of the arrival.

'You've got to come home with me, Lou,' Mrs. Higgins began, as she wiped her perspiring face. 'I've promised to have you back by this afternoon. Dada's right down angry; you wouldn't know him. He blames everything on to you, and you'd better just come home quiet.'

'I shall do nothing of the kind,' answered Louise, her temper rising.

Mrs. Higgins glared at her and began to rail; the voice was painfully audible to Emmeline, who just then passed through the hall. Miss Derrick gave as good as she received; a battle raged for some minutes, differing from many a former conflict only in the moderation of pitch and vocabulary due to their being in a stranger's house.

'Then you won't come?' cried the mother at length. 'I've had my journey for nothing, have I? Then just go and fetch Mrs. What's–her–name. She must hear what I've got to say.'

'Mrs. Mumford isn't at home,' answered Louise, with bold mendacity. 'And a very good thing too. I should be sorry for her to see you in the state you're in.'

'I'm in no more of a state than you are, Louise! And just you listen to this. Not one farthing more will you have from 'ome — not one farthing! And you may think yourself lucky if you still 'ave a 'ome. For all I know, you'll have to earn your own living, and I'd like to hear how you mean to do it. As soon as I get back I shall write to Mrs. What's–her–name and tell her that nothing will be paid for you after the week that's due and the week that's for notice. Now just take heed of what you're doing, Lou. It may have more serious results than you think for.'

'I've thought all I'm going to think,' replied the girl. '[shall stay here as long as I like, and be indebted neither to you nor to stepfather.'

33

Mrs. Mumford breathed a sigh of thankfulness that she was not called upon to take part in this scene. It was bad enough that the servant engaged in laying lunch could hear distinctly Mrs. Higgins's coarse and violent onslaught. When the front door at length closed she rejoiced, but with trembling; for the words that fell upon her ear from the hall announced too plainly that Louise was determined to stay.

CHAPTER V

Miss Derrick had gone back into the drawing-room, and, to Emmeline's surprise, remained there. This retirement was ominous; the girl must be taking some resolve. Emmeline, on her part, braced her courage for the step on which she had decided. Luncheon awaited them, but it would be much better to arrive at an understanding before they sat down to the meal. She entered the room and found Louise leaning on the back of a chair.

'I dare say you heard the row,' Miss Derrick remarked coldly. 'I'm very sorry, but nothing of that kind shall happen again.'

Her countenance was disturbed, she seemed to be putting a restraint upon herself, and only with great effort to subdue her voice.

'What are you going to do?' asked Emmeline, in a friendly tone, but, as it were, from a distance.

'I am going to ask you to do me a great kindness, Mrs. Mumford.'

There was no reply. The girl paused a moment, then resumed impulsively.

'Mr. Higgins says that if I don't come home, he won't let me have any more money. They're going to write and tell you that they won't be responsible after this for my board and lodging. Of course I shall not go home; I shouldn't dream of it; I'd rather earn my living as — as a scullery maid. I want to ask you, Mrs. Mumford, whether you will let me stay on, and trust me to pay what I owe you. It won't be for very long, and I promise you I will pay, every penny.'

The Paying Guest

The natural impulse of Emmeline's disposition was to reply with hospitable kindliness; she found it very difficult to maintain her purpose; it shamed her to behave like the ordinary landlady, to appear actuated by mean motives. But the domestic strain was growing intolerable, and she felt sure that Clarence would be exasperated if her weakness prolonged it.

'Now do let me advise you, Louise,' she answered gently. 'Are you acting wisely? Wouldn't it be very much better to go home?',

Louise lost all her self-control. Flushed with anger, her eyes glaring, she broke into vehement exclamations.

'You want to get rid of me! Very well, I'll go this moment. I was going to tell you something; but you don't care what becomes of me. I'll send for my luggage; you shan't be troubled with it long. And you'll be paid all that's owing. I didn't think you were one of that kind. I'll go this minute.'

'Just as you please,' said Emmeline, 'Your temper is really so very——'

'Oh, I know. It's always my temper, and nobody else is ever to blame. I wouldn't stay another night in the house, if I had to sleep on the Downs!'

She flung out of the room and flew upstairs. Emmeline, angered by this unwarrantable treatment, determined to hold aloof, and let the girl do as she would. Miss Derrick was of full age, and quite capable of taking care of herself, or at all events ought to be. Perhaps this was the only possible issue of the difficulties in which they had all become involved; neither Louise nor her parents could be dealt with in the rational, peaceful way preferred by well-conditioned people. To get her out of the house was the main point; if she chose to depart in a whirlwind, that was her own affair. All but certainly she would go home, to-morrow if not to-day.

In less than a quarter of an hour her step sounded on the stairs — would she turn into the dining-room, where Emmeline now sat at table? No; straight through the hall, and out at the front door, which closed, however, quite softly behind her. That she did not slam it seemed wonderful to Emmeline. The girl was not wholly a savage.

The Paying Guest

Presently Mrs. Mumford went up to inspect the forsaken chamber. Louise had packed all her things: of course she must have tumbled them recklessly into the trunks. Drawers were left open, as if to exhibit their emptiness, but in other respects the room looked tidy enough. Neatness and order came by no means naturally to Miss Derrick, and Emmeline did not know what pains the girl had taken, ever since her arrival, to live in conformity with the habits of a 'nice' household.

Louise, meanwhile, had gone to the railway station, intending to take a ticket for Victoria. But half an hour must elapse before the arrival of a train, and she walked about in an irresolute mood. For one thing, she felt hungry; at Sutton her appetite had been keen, and meal–times were always welcome. She entered the refreshment room, and with inward murmurs made a repast which reminded her of the excellent luncheon she might now have been enjoying. All the time, she pondered her situation. Ultimately, instead of booking for Victoria, she procured a ticket for Epsom Downs, and had not long to wait for the train.

It was a hot day at the end of June. Wafts of breezy coolness passed now and then over the high open country, but did not suffice to combat the sun's steady glare. After walking half a mile or so, absorbed in thought, Louise suffered so much that she looked about for shadow. Before her was the towering ugliness of the Grand Stand; this she had seen and admired when driving past it with her friends; it did not now attract her. In another direction the Downs were edged with trees, and that way she turned. All but overcome with heat and weariness, she at length found a shaded spot where her solitude seemed secure. And, after seating herself, the first thing she did was to have a good cry.

Then for an hour she sat thinking, and as she thought her face gradually emerged from gloom — the better, truer face which so often allowed itself to be disguised at the prompting of an evil spirit; her softening lips all but smiled, as if at an amusing suggestion, and her eyes, in their reverie, seemed to behold a pleasant promise. Unconsciously she plucked and tasted the sweet stems of grass that grew about her. At length, the sun's movements having robbed her of shadow, she rose, looked at her watch, and glanced around for another retreat. Hard by was a little wood, delightfully grassy and cool, fenced about with railings she could easily have climbed; but a notice–board, severely admonishing trespassers, forbade the attempt. With a petulant remark to herself on the selfishness of "those people," she sauntered past.

The Paying Guest

Along this edge of the Downs stands a picturesque row of pine–trees, stunted, bittered, and twisted through many a winter by the upland gales. Louise noticed them, only to think for a moment what ugly trees they were. Before her, east, west, and north, lay the wooded landscape, soft of hue beneath the summer sky, spreading its tranquil beauty far away to the mists of the horizon. In vivacious company she would have called it, and perhaps have thought it, a charming view; alone, she had no eye for such things — an indifference characteristic of her mind, and not at all dependent upon its mood. Presently another patch of shade invited her to repose again, and again she meditated for an hour or more.

The sun had grown less ardent, and a breeze, no longer fitful, made walking pleasant. The sight of holiday–making school-children, who, in their ribboned hats and white pinafores, were having tea not far away, suggested to Louise that she also would like such refreshment. Doubtless it might be procured at the inn yonder, near the racecourse, and thither she began to move. Her thoughts were more at rest; she had made her plan for the evening; all that had to be done was to kill time for another hour or so. Walking lightly over the turf, she noticed the chalk marks significant of golf, and wondered how the game was played. Without difficulty she obtained her cup of tea, loitered over it as long as possible, strayed yet awhile about the Downs, and towards half–past six made for the railway station.

She travelled no further than Sutton, and there lingered in the waiting room till the arrival of a certain train from London Bridge. As the train came in she took up a position near the exit. Among the people who had alighted, her eye soon perceived Clarence Mumford. She stepped up to him and drew his attention.

'Oh! have you come by the same train?' he asked, shaking hands with her.

'No. I've been waiting here because I wanted to see you, Mr. Mumford. Will you spare me a minute or two?'

'Here? In the station?'

'Please — if you don't mind.'

The Paying Guest

Astonished, Mumford drew aside with her to a quiet part of the long platform. Louise, keeping a very grave countenance, told him rapidly all that had befallen since his departure from home in the morning.

'I behaved horridly, and I was sorry for it as soon as I had left the house. After all Mrs. Mumford's kindness to me, and yours, I don't know how I could be so horrid. But the quarrel with mother had upset me so, and I felt so miserable when Mrs. Mumford seemed to want to get rid of me. I feel sure she didn't really want to send me away: she was only advising me, as she thought, for my good. But I can't, and won't, go home. And I've been waiting all the afternoon to see you. No; not here. I went to Epsom Downs and walked about, and then came back just in time. And — do you think I might go back? I don't mean now, at once, but this evening, after you've had dinner. I really don't know where to go for the night, and it's such a stupid position to be in, isn't it?'

With perfect naïveté, or with perfect simulation of it, she looked him in the face, and it was Mumford who had to avert his eyes. The young man felt very uncomfortable.

'Oh! I'm quite sure Emmy will be glad to let you come for the night, Miss Derrick———'

'Yes, but — Mr. Mumford, I want to stay longer — a few weeks longer. Do you think Mrs. Mumford would forgive me? I have made up my mind what to do, and I ought to have told her. I should have, if I hadn't lost my temper.'

'Well,' replied the other, in grave embarrassment, but feeling that he had no alternative, 'let us go to the house———'

'Oh! I couldn't. I shouldn't like anyone to know that I spoke to you about it. It wouldn't be nice, would it? I thought if I came later, after dinner. And perhaps you could talk to Mrs. Mumford, and — and prepare her. I mean, perhaps you wouldn't mind saying you were sorry I had gone so suddenly. And then perhaps Mrs. Mumford — she's so kind — would say that she was sorry too. And then I might come into the garden and find you both sitting there———'

Mumford, despite his most uneasy frame of mind, betrayed a passing amusement. He looked into the girl's face and saw its prettiness flush with pretty confusion, and this did not tend to restore his tranquillity.

The Paying Guest

'What shall you do in the meantime?'

'Oh! go into the town and have something to eat, and then walk about.'

'You must be dreadfully tired already.'

'Just a little; but I don't mind. It serves me right. I shall be so grateful to you, Mr. Mumford. If you won't let me come, I suppose I must go to London and ask one of my friends to take me in.'

'I will arrange it. Come about half–past eight. We shall be in the garden by then.'

Avoiding her look, he moved away and ran up the stairs. But from the exit of the station he walked slowly, in part to calm himself, to assume his ordinary appearance, and in part to think over the comedy he was going to play.

Emmeline met him at the door, herself too much flurried to notice anything peculiar in her husband's aspect. She repeated the story with which he was already acquainted.

'And really, after all, I am so glad!' was her conclusion. 'I didn't think she had really gone; all the afternoon I've been expecting to see her back again. But she won't come now, and it is a good thing to have done with the wretched business. I only hope she will tell the truth to her people. She might say that we turned her out of the house. But I don't think so; in spite of all her faults, she never seemed deceitful or malicious.'

Mumford was strongly tempted to reveal what had happened at the station, but he saw danger alike in disclosure and in reticence.

When there enters the slightest possibility of jealousy, a man can never be sure that his wife will act as a rational being. He feared to tell the simple truth lest Emmeline should not believe his innocence of previous plotting with Miss Derrick, or at all events should be irritated by the circumstances into refusing Louise a lodging for the night. And with no less apprehension he decided at length to keep the secret, which might so easily become known hereafter, and would then have such disagreeable consequences.

'Well, let us have dinner, Emmy; I'm hungry. Yes, it's a good thing she has gone; but I wish it hadn't happened in that way. What a spitfire she is!'

'I never, never saw the like. And if you had heard Mrs. Higgins! Oh, what dreadful people! Clarence, hear me register a vow——'

'It was my fault, dear. I'm awfully sorry I got you in for such horrors. It was wholly and entirely my fault.'

By due insistence on this, Mumford of course put his wife into an excellent humour, and, after they had dined, she returned to her regret that the girl should have gone so suddenly. Clarence, declaring that he would allow himself a cigar, instead of the usual pipe, to celebrate the restoration of domestic peace, soon led Emmeline into the garden.

'Heavens! how hot it has been. Eighty–five in our office at noon — eighty–five! Fellows are discarding waistcoats and wearing what they call a cummerbund — silk sash round the waist. I think I must follow the fashion. How should I look, do you think?'

'You don't really mind that we lose the money?' Emmeline asked presently.

'Pooh! We shall do well enough. — Who's that?'

Someone was entering the garden by the side path. And in a moment there remained no doubt who the person was. Louise came forward, her head bent, her features eloquent of fatigue and distress.

'Mrs. Mumford — I couldn't — without asking you to forgive me——'

Her voice broke with a sob. She stood in a humble attitude, and Emmeline, though pierced with vexation, had no choice but to hold out a welcoming hand.

'Have you come all the way back from London just to say this?'

'I haven't been to London. I've walked about — all day — and oh, I'm so tired and miserable! Will you let me stay, just for to–night? I shall be so grateful.'

'Of course you may stay, Miss Derrick. It was very far from my wish to see you go off at a moment's notice. But I really couldn't stop you.'

Mumford had stepped aside, out of hearing. He forgot his private embarrassment in speculation as to the young woman's character. That she was acting distress and penitence he could hardly believe; indeed, there was no necessity to accuse her of dishonest behaviour. The trivial concealment between him and her amounted to nothing, did not alter the facts of the situation. But what could be at the root of her seemingly so foolish existence? Emmeline held to the view that she was in love with the man Cobb, though perhaps unwilling to admit it, even in her own silly mind. It might be so, and, if so, it made her more interesting; for one was tempted to think that Louise had not the power of loving at all. Yet, for his own part, he couldn't help liking her; the eyes at had looked into his at the station haunted him a little, and would not let him think of her contemptuously. But what a woman to make ones wife! Unless — unless——

Louise had gone into the house. Emmeline approached her husband.

'There! I foresaw it. Isn't vexing?'

'Never mind, dear. She'll go to morrow, or the day after.'

'I wish I could be sure of that.'

CHAPTER VI

Louise did not appear again that evening. Thoroughly tired, she unpacked her trunks, sat awhile by the open window, listening to a piano in a neighbouring house, and then jumped into bed. From ten o'clock to eight next morning she slept soundly.

At breakfast her behaviour was marked with excessive decorum. To the ordinary civilities of her host and hostess she replied softly, modestly, in the manner of a very young and timid girl; save when addressed, she kept silence, and sat with head inclined; a virginal freshness breathed about her; she ate very little, and that without her usual gusto, but rather as if performing a dainty ceremony. Her eyes never moved in Mumford's direction.

The Paying Guest

The threatened letter from Mrs. Higgins had arrived; Emmeline and her husband read it before their guest came down. If Louise continued to reside with them, they entertained her with a full knowledge that no payment must be expected from Coburg Lodge. Emmeline awaited the disclosure of her guest's project, which had more than once been alluded to yesterday; she could not dream of permitting Louise to stay for more than a day or two, whatever the suggestion offered. This morning she had again heard from her sister, Mrs. Grove, who was strongly of opinion that Miss Derrick should be sent back to her native sphere.

'I shall always feel,' she said to her husband, 'that we have behaved badly. I was guilty of false pretences. Fortunately, we have the excuse of her unbearable temper. But for that, I should feel dreadfully ashamed of myself.'

Very soon after Mumford's departure, Louise begged for a few minutes' private talk.

'Every time I come into this drawing–room, Mrs. Mumford, I think how pretty it is. What pains you must have taken in furnishing it! I never saw such nice curtains anywhere else. And that little screen — I am so fond of that screen!'

'It was a wedding present from an old friend,' Emmeline replied, complacently regarding the object, which shone with embroidery of many colours.

'Will you help me when I furnish my drawing–room?' Louise asked sweetly. And she added, with a direct look, 'I don't think it will be very long.'

'Indeed?'

'I am going to marry Mr. Bowling.'

Emmeline could no longer fed astonishment at anything her guest said or did. The tone, the air, with which Louise made this declaration affected her with a sense of something quite unforeseen; but, at the same time, she asked herself why she had not foreseen it. Was not this the obvious answer to the riddle? All along, Louise had wished to marry Mr. Bowling. She might or might not have consciously helped to bring about the rupture between Mr. Bowling and Miss Higgins; she might, or might not, have felt genuinely reluctant to take advantage of her half–sister's defeat. But a struggle had been going on in the girl's conscience, at all events. Yes, this explained everything. And, on the whole, it seemed to speak in Louise's favour. Her ridicule of Mr. Bowling's person and character became, in this new light, a proof of desire to resist her inclinations. She had only yielded when it was certain that Miss Higgins's former lover had quite thrown off his old allegiance, and when no good could be done by self–sacrifice.

'When did you make up your mind to this, Louise?'

'Yesterday, after our horrid quarrel. No, you didn't quarrel; it was all my abominable temper. This morning I'm going to answer Mr. Bowling's last letter, and I shall tell him — what I've told you. He'll be delighted!'

'Then you have really wished for this from the first?'

Louise plucked at the fringe on the arm of her chair, and replied at length with maidenly frankness.

'I always thought it would be a good marriage for me. But I never — do believe me — I never tried to cut Cissy out. The truth is I thought a good deal of the other — of Mr. Cobb. But I knew that I couldn't marry him. It would be dreadful; we should quarrel frightfully, and he would kill me — I feel sure he would, he's so violent in his temper. But Mr. Bowling is very nice; he couldn't get angry if he tried. And ho has a much better position than Mr. Cobb.'

Emmeline began to waver in her conviction and to feel a natural annoyance.

'And you think,' she said coldly, 'that your marriage will take place soon?'

'That's what I want to speak about, dear Mrs. Mumford. Did you hear from my mother this morning? Then you see what my position is. I am homeless. If I leave you, I don't know where I shall go. When Mr. Higgins knows I'm going to. marry Mr. Bowling he won't have me in the house, even if I wanted to go back. Cissy Will be furious: she'll come back from Margate just to keep up her father's anger against me. If you could let me stay here just a short time, Mrs. Mumford; just a few weeks I should so like to be married from your house.'

The Paying Guest

The listener trembled with irritation, and before she could command her voice Louise added eagerly:

'Of course, when we're married, Mr. Bowling will pay all my debts.'

"You are quite mistaken,' said Emmeline distantly, 'if you think that the money matter has anything to do with — with my unreadiness to agree——'

'Oh, I didn't think it — not for a moment. I'm a trouble to you; I know I am. But I'll be so quiet, dear Mrs. Mumford. You shall hardly know I'm in the house. If once it's all settled I shall never be out of temper. Do, please, let me stay! I like you so much, and how wretched it would be if I had to be married from a lodging–house.'

'I'm afraid, Louise — I'm really afraid——'

'Of my temper?' the girl interrupted. 'If ever I say an angry word you shall turn me out that very moment. Dear Mrs. Mumford! Oh! what shall I do if you won't be kind to me? What will become of me? I have no home, and everybody hates me.'

'Tears streamed down her face; she lay back, overcome with misery. Emmeline was distracted. She felt herself powerless to act as common–sense dictated, yet desired more than ever to rid herself of every shadow of responsibility for the girl's proceedings. The idea of this marriage taking place at "Runnymede" made her blood run cold. No, no; that was absolutely out of the question. But equally impossible did it seem to speak with brutal decision. Once more she must temporise, and hope for courage on another day.

'I can't — I really can't give you a definite answer till I have spoken with Mr. Mumford.'

'Oh! I am sure he will do me this kindness,' sobbed Louise.

A slight emphasis on the "he" touched Mrs. Mumford unpleasantly. She rose, and began to pick out some overblown flowers from a vase on the table near her. Presently Louise became silent. Before either of them spoke again a postman's knock sounded at the house–door, and Emmeline went to see what letter had been delivered. It was for Miss Derrick; the handwriting, as Emmeline knew, that of Mr. Cobb.

44

The Paying Guest

'Oh, bother!' Louise murmured, as she took the letter from Mrs. Mumford's hand. 'Well, I'm a trouble to everybody, and I don't know how it'll all end. I daresay I shan't live very long.'

'Don't talk nonsense, Louise.'

'Should you like me to go at once, Mrs. Mumford?' the girl asked, with a submissive sigh.

'No, no. Let us think over it for a day or two. Perhaps you haven't quite made up your mind, after all.'

To this, oddly enough, Louise gave no reply. She lingered by the window, nervously bending and rolling her letter, which she did not seem to think of opening. After a glance or two of discreet curiosity, Mrs. Mumford left the room. Daily duties called for attention, and she was not at all inclined to talk further with Louise. The girl, as soon as she found herself alone, broke Mr. Cobb's envelope, which contained four sides of bold handwriting — not a long letter, but, as usual, vigorously worded. 'Dear Miss Derrick,' he wrote, 'I haven't been in a hurry to reply to your last, as it seemed to me that you were in one of your touchy moods when you sent it. It wasn't my fault that I called at the house when you were away. I happened to have business at Croydon unexpectedly, and ran over to Sutton just on the chance of seeing you. And I have no objection to tell you all I said to your friend there. I am not in the habit of saying things behind people's backs that I don't wish them to hear. All I did was to ask out plainly whether Mrs. M. was trying to persuade you to have nothing to do with me. She said she wasn't, and that she didn't wish to interfere one way or another. I told her that I could ask no more than that. She seemed to me a sensible sort of woman, and I don't suppose you'll get much harm from her, though I daresay she thinks more about dress and amusements, and so on, than is good for her or anyone else. You say at the end of your letter that I'm to let you know when I think of coming again, and if you mean by that that you would be glad to see me, I can only say, thank you. I don't mean to give you up yet, and I don't believe you want me to say what you will. I don't spy after you; you're mistaken in that. But I'm pretty much always thinking about you, and I wish you were nearer to me. I may have to go to Bristol in a week or two, and perhaps I shall be there for a month or more, so I must see you before then. Will you tell me what day would suit you, after seven? If you don't want me to come to the house, then meet me where you like. And there's only one more thing I have to say — you must deal honestly with me. I can wait, but I won't be deceived.'

45

The Paying Guest

Louise pondered for a long time, turning now to this part of the letter, now to that. And the lines of her face, though they made no approach to smiling, indicated agreeable thoughts. Tears had left just sufficient trace to give her meditations a semblance of unwonted seriousness.

About midday she went up to her room and wrote letters. The first was to Miss Cissy Higgins: — 'Dear Ciss, — I dare say you would like to know that Mr. B. has proposed to me. If you have any objection, please let me know it by return. — Affectionately yours, L. E. DERRICK.' This she addressed to Margate, and stamped with a little thump of the fist. Her next sheet of paper was devoted to Mr. Bowling, and the letter, though brief, cost her some thought. 'Dear Mr. Bowling, — Your last is so very nice and kind that I feel I ought to answer it without delay, but I cannot answer in the way you wish. I must have a long, long time to think over such a very important question. I don't blame you in the least for your behaviour to someone we know of; and I think, after all that happened, you were quite free. It is quite true that she did not behave straightforwardly, and I am very sorry to have to say it. I shall not be going home again: I have quite made up my mind about that. I am afraid I must not let you come here to call upon me. I have a particular reason for it. To tell you the truth, my friend Mrs. Mumford is very particular, and rather fussy, and has a rather trying temper. So please do not come just yet. I am quite well, and enjoying myself in a very quiet way. — I remain, sincerely yours, LOUISE E. DERRICK.' Finally she penned a reply to Mr. Cobb, and this, after a glance at a railway time–table, gave her no trouble at all. 'Dear Mr. Cobb,' she scribbled, 'if you really must see me before you go away to Bristol, or wherever it is, you had better meet me on Saturday at Streatham Station, which is about halfway between me and you. I shall come by the train from Sutton, which reaches Streatham at 8.6. — Yours truly, L. E. D.'

To–day was Thursday. When Saturday came the state of things at "Runnymede" had undergone no change whatever; Emmeline still waited for a moment of courage, and Mumford, though he did not relish the prospect, began to think it more than probable that Miss Derrick would hold her ground until her actual marriage with Mr. Bowling. Whether that unknown person would discharge the debt his betrothed was incurring seemed an altogether uncertain matter. Louise, in the meantime, kept quiet as a mouse — so strangely quiet, indeed, that Emmeline's prophetic soul dreaded some impending disturbance, worse than any they had yet suffered.

The Paying Guest

At luncheon, Louise made known that she would have to leave in the middle of dinner to catch a train. No explanation was offered or asked, but Emmeline, it being Saturday, said she would put the dinner–hour earlier, to suit her friend's convenience. Louise smiled pleasantly, and said how very kind it was of Mrs. Mumford.

She had no difficulty in reaching Streatham by the time appointed. Unfortunately, it was a cloudy evening, and a spattering of rain fell from time to time.

'I suppose you'll be afraid to walk to the Common,' said Mr. Cobb, who stood waiting at the exit from the station, and showed more satisfaction in his countenance when Louise appeared than he evinced in words.

'Oh, I don't care,' she answered. 'It won't rain much, and I've brought my umbrella, and I've nothing on that will take any harm.'

She had, indeed, dressed herself in her least demonstrative costume. Cobb wore the usual garb of his leisure hours, which was better than that in which he had called the other day at "Runnymede." For some minutes they walked towards Streatham Common without interchange of a word, and with no glance at each other. Then the man coughed, and said bluntly that he was glad Louise had come.

'Well, I wanted to see you,' was her answer.

'What about?'

'I don't think I shall be able to stay with the Mumfords. They're very nice people, but they're not exactly my sort, and we don't get on very well. Where had I better go?'

'Go? Why home, of course. The best place for you.'

Cobb was prepared for a hot retort, but it did not come. After a moment's reflection, Louise said quietly:

'I can't go home. I've quarrelled with them too badly. You haven't seen mother lately? Then I must tell you how things are.'

The Paying Guest

She did so, with no concealment save of the correspondence with Mr. Bowling, and the not unimportant statements concerning him which she had made to Mrs. Mumford. In talking with Cobb, Louise seemed to drop a degree or so in social status; her language was much less careful than when she conversed with the Mumfords, and even her voice struck a note of less refinement. Decidedly she was more herself, if that could be said of one who very rarely made conscious disguise of her characteristics.

'Better stay where you are, then, for the present,' said Cobb, when he had listened attentively. 'I dare say you can get along well enough with the people, if you try.'

'That's all very well; but what about paying them? I shall owe three guineas for every week I stop.'

'It's a great deal, and they ought to feed you very well for it,' replied the other, smiling rather sourly.

'Don't be vulgar. I suppose you think I ought to live on a few shillings a week.'

'Lots of people have to. But there's no reason why you should. But look here: why should you be quarrelling with your people now about that fellow Bowling? You don't see him anywhere, do you?'

He flashed a glance at her, and Louise answered with a defiant motion of the head.

'No, I don't. But they put the blame on me, all the same. I shouldn't wonder if they think I'm trying to get him.'

She opened her umbrella, for heavy drops had begun to fall; they pattered on Cobb's hard felt hat, and Louise tried to shelter him as well as herself.

'Never mind me,' he said. 'And here, let me hold that thing over you. If you just put your arm in mine, it'll be easier. That's the way. Take two steps to my one; that's it.'

Again they were silent for a few moments. They had reached the Common, and Cobb struck along a path most likely to be unfrequented. No wind was blowing; the rain fell in steady spots that could all but be counted, and the air grew dark.

'Well, I can only propose one thing,' sounded the masculine voice. 'You can get out of it by marrying me.'

Louise gave a little laugh, rather timid than scornful.

'Yes, I suppose I can. But it's an awkward way. It would be rather like using a sledge–hammer to crack a nut.'

'It'll come sooner or later,' asserted Cobb, with genial confidence.

'That's what I don't like about you.' Louise withdrew her arm petulantly. 'You always speak as if I couldn't help myself. Don't you suppose I have any choice?'

'Plenty, no doubt,' was the grim answer.

'Whenever we begin to quarrel it's your fault,' pursued Miss Derrick, with unaccustomed moderation of tone. 'I never knew a man who behaved like you do. You seem to think the way to make anyone like you is to bully them. We should have got on very much better if you had tried to be pleasant.'

'I don't think we've got along badly, all things considered,' Cobb replied, as if after weighing a doubt. 'We'd a good deal rather be together than apart, it seems to me; or else, why do we keep meeting? And I don't want to bully anybody — least of all, you. It's a way I have of talking, I suppose. You must judge a man by his actions and his meaning, not by the tone of his voice. You know very well what a great deal I think of you. Of course I don't like it when you begin to speak as if you were only playing with me; nobody would.'

'I'm serious enough,' said Louise, trying to hold the umbrella over her companion, and only succeeding in directing moisture down the back of his neck. 'And it's partly through you that I've got into such difficulties.'

'How do you make that out?'

'If it wasn't for you, I should very likely marry Mr. Bowling.'

The Paying Guest

'Oh, he's asked you, has he?' cried Cobb, staring at her. 'Why didn't you tell me that before? — Don't let me stand in your way. I dare say he's just the kind of man for you. At all events, he's like you in not knowing his own mind.'

'Go on! Go on!' Louise exclaimed carelessly. 'There's plenty of time. Say all you've got to say.'

From the gloom of the eastward sky came a rattling of thunder, like quick pistol–shots. Cobb checked his steps.

'We mustn't go any further. You're getting wet, and the rain isn't likely to stop.'

'I shall not go back,' Louise answered, 'until something has been settled.' And she stood before him, her eyes cast down, whilst Cobb looked at the darkening sky. 'I want to know what's going to become of me. The Mumfords won't keep me much longer, and I don't wish to stay where I'm not wanted.'

'Let us walk down the hill.'

A flash of lightning made Louise start, and the thunder rattled again. But only light drops were falling. The girl stood her ground.

'I want to know what I am to do. If you can't help me, say so, and let me go my own way.'

'Of course I can help you. That is, if you'll be honest with me. I want to know, first of all, whether you've been encouraging that man Bowling.'

'No, I haven't.'

'Very well, I believe you. And now I'll make you a fair offer. Marry me as soon as I can make the arrangements, and I'll pay all you owe, and see that you are in comfortable lodgings until I've time to get a house. It could be done before I go to Bristol, and then, of course, you could go with me.'

'You speak,' said Louise, after a short silence, 'just as if you were making an agreement with a servant.'

50

The Paying Guest

'That's all nonsense, and you know it. I've told you how I think, often enough, in letters, and I'm not good at saying it. Look here, I don't think it's very wise to stand out in the middle of the Common in a thunderstorm. Let us walk on, and I think I would put down your umbrella.'

'It wouldn't trouble you much if I were struck with lightning.'

'All right, take it so. I shan't trouble to contradict.'

Louise followed his advice, and they began to walk quickly down the slope towards Streatham. Neither spoke until they were in the high road again. A strong wind was driving the rain−clouds to other regions and the thunder had ceased; there came a grey twilight; rows of lamps made a shimmering upon the wet ways.

'What sort of a house would you take?' Louise asked suddenly.

'Oh, a decent enough house. What kind do you want?'

'Something like the Mumfords'. It needn't be quite so large,' she added quickly; 'but a house with a garden, in a nice road, and in a respectable part.'

'That would suit me well enough,' answered Cobb cheerfully. 'You seem to think I want to drag you down, but you're very much mistaken. I'm doing pretty well, and likely, as far as I can see, to do better. I don't grudge you money; far from it. All I want to know is, that you'll marry me for my own sake.'

He dropped his voice, not to express tenderness, but because other people were near. Upon Louise, however, it had a pleasing effect, and she smiled.

'Very well,' she made answer, in the same subdued tone. 'Then let us settle it in that way.'

They talked amicably for the rest of the time that they spent together. It was nearly an hour, and never before had they succeeded in conversing so long without a quarrel. Louise became light−hearted and mirthful; her companion, though less abandoned to the mood of the moment, wore a hopeful countenance. Through all his roughness, Cobb was distinguished by a personal delicacy which no doubt had impressed Louise, say what she

51

might of pretended fears. At parting, he merely shook hands with her, as always.

CHAPTER VII

Glad of a free evening, Emmeline, after dinner, walked round to Mrs. Fentiman's. Louise had put a restraint upon the wonted friendly intercourse between the Mumfords and their only familiar acquaintances at Sutton. Mrs. Fentiman liked to talk of purely domestic matters, and in a stranger's presence she was never at ease. Coming alone, and when the children were all safe in bed, Emmeline had a warm welcome. For the first time she spoke of her troublesome guest without reserve. This chat would have been restful and enjoyable but for a most unfortunate remark that fell from the elder lady, a perfectly innocent mention of something her husband had told her, but, secretly, so disturbing Mrs. Mumford that, after hearing it, she got away as soon as possible, and walked quickly home with dark countenance.

It was ten o'clock; Louise had not yet returned, but might do so any moment. Wishing to be sure of privacy in a conversation with her husband, Emmeline summoned him from his book to the bedroom.

'Well, what has happened now?' exclaimed Mumford. 'If this kind of thing goes on much longer I shall feel inclined to take a lodging in town.'

'I have heard something very strange. I can hardly believe it; there must have been a mistake.'

'What is it? Really, one's nerves——'

'Is it true that, on Thursday evening, you and Miss Derrick were seen talking together at the station? Thursday: the day she went off and came back again after dinner.'

Mumford would gladly have got out of this scrape at any expense of mendacity, but he saw at once how useless such an attempt would prove. Exasperated by the result of his indiscretion, and resenting, as all men do, the undignified necessity of defending himself, he flew into a rage. Yes, it was true, and what next? The girl had waylaid him, begged him to intercede for her with his wife. Of course it would have been better to come home and reveal the matter; he didn't do so because it seemed to put him in a silly position. For Heaven's sake, let the whole absurd business be forgotten and done with!

Emmeline, though not sufficiently enlightened to be above small jealousies, would have been ashamed to declare her feeling with the energy of unsophisticated female nature. She replied coldly and loftily that the matter, of course, was done with; that it interested her no more; but that she could not help regretting an instance of secretiveness such as she had never before discovered in her husband. Surely he had put himself in a much sillier position, as things turned out, than if he had followed the dictates of honour.

'The upshot of it is this,' cried Mumford: 'Miss Derrick has to leave the house, and, if necessary, I shall tell her so myself.'

Again Emmeline was cold and lofty. There was no necessity whatever for any further communication between Clarence and Miss Derrick. Let the affair be left entirely in her hands. Indeed, she must very specially request that Clarence would have nothing more to do with Miss Derrick's business. Whereupon Mumford took offence. Did Emmeline wish to imply that there had been anything improper in his behaviour beyond the paltry indiscretion to which he had confessed? No; Emmeline was thankful to say that she did not harbour base suspicions. Then, rejoined Mumford, let this be the last word of a difference as hateful to him as to her. And he left the room.

His wife did not linger more than a minute behind him, and she sat in the drawing–room to await Miss Derrick's return; Mumford kept apart in what was called the library. To her credit, Emmeline tried hard to believe that she had learnt the whole truth; her mind, as she had justly declared, was not prone to ignoble imaginings; but acquitting her husband by no means involved an equal charity towards Louise. Hitherto uncertain in her judgment, she had now the relief of an assurance that Miss Derrick was not at all a proper person to entertain as a guest, on whatever terms. The incident of the railway station proved her to be utterly lacking in self–respect, in feminine modesty, even if her behaviour merited no darker description. Emmeline could now face with confidence the scene from which she had shrunk; not only was it a duty to insist upon Miss Derrick's departure, it would be a positive pleasure.

Louise very soon entered; she came into the room with her brightest look, and cried gaily:

The Paying Guest

'Oh, I hope I haven't kept you waiting for me. Are you alone?'

'No. I have been out.'

'Had you the storm here? I'm not going to keep you talking; you look tired.'

'I am rather,' said Emmeline, with reserve. She had no intention of allowing Louise to suspect the real cause of what she was about to say — that would have seemed to her undignified; but she could not speak quite naturally. 'Still, I should be glad if you would sit down for a minute.'

The girl took a chair and began to draw off her gloves. She understood what was coming; it appeared in Emmeline's face.

'Something to say to me, Mrs. Mumford?'

'I hope you won't think me unkind. I feel obliged to ask you when you will be able to make new arrangements.'

'You would like me to go soon?' said Louise, inspecting her finger-nails, and speaking without irritation.

'I am sorry to say that I think it better you should leave us. Forgive this plain speaking, Miss Derrick. It's always best to be perfectly straightforward, isn't it?'

Whether she felt the force of this innuendo or not, Louise took it in good part. As if the idea had only just struck her, she looked up cheerfully.

'You're quite right, Mrs. Mumford. I'm sure you've been very kind to me, and I've had a very pleasant time here, but it wouldn't do for me to stay longer. May I wait over to-morrow, just till Wednesday morning, to have an answer to a letter?'

'Certainly, if it is quite understood that there will be no delay beyond that. There are circumstances — private matters — I don't feel quite able to explain. But I must be sure that you will have left us by Wednesday afternoon.'

The Paying Guest

'You may be sure of it. I will write a line and post it to-night, for it to go as soon as possible.'

Therewith Louise stood up and, smiling, withdrew. Emmeline was both relieved and surprised; she had not thought it possible for the girl to conduct herself at such a juncture with such perfect propriety. An outbreak of ill-temper, perhaps of insolence, had seemed more than likely; at best she looked for tears and entreaties. Well, it was over, and by Wednesday the house would be restored to its ancient calm. Ancient, indeed! One could not believe that so short a time had passed since Miss Derrick first entered the portals. Only one more day.

'Oh, blindness to the future, kindly given, That each may fill the circle marked by Heaven.' At school, Emmeline had learnt and recited these lines; but it was long since they had recurred to her memory.

In ten minutes Louise had written her letter. She went out, returned, and looked in at the drawing-room, with a pleasant smile. 'Good-night, Mrs. Mumford.' 'Good-night, Miss Derrick.' For the grace of the thing, Emmeline would have liked to say 'Louise,' but could not bring her lips to utter the name.

About a year ago there had been a little misunderstanding between Mr. and Mrs. Mumford, which lasted for some twenty-four hours, during which they had nothing to say to each other. To-night they found themselves in a similar situation, and remembered that last difference, and wondered, both of them, at the harmony of their married life. It was in truth wonderful enough; twelve months without a shadow of ill-feeling between them. The reflection compelled Mumford to speak when his head was on the pillow.

'Emmy, we're making fools of ourselves. Just tell me what you have done.'

'I can't see how I am guilty of foolishness,' was the clear-cut reply.

'Then why are you angry with me?'

'I don't like deceit.'

'Hanged if I don't dislike it just as much. When is that girl going?'

The Paying Guest

Emmeline made known the understanding at which she had arrived, and her husband breathed an exclamation of profound thankfulness. But peace was not perfectly restored.

In another room, Louise lay communing with her thoughts, which were not at all disagreeable. She had written to Cobb, telling him what had happened, and asking him to let her know by Wednesday morning what she was to do. She could not go home; he must not bid her do so; but she would take a lodging wherever he liked. The position seemed romantic and enjoyable. Not till after her actual marriage should the people at home know what had become of her. She was marrying with utter disregard of all her dearest ambitions all the same, she had rather be the wife of Cobb than of anyone else. Her stepfather might recover his old kindness and generosity as soon as he knew she no longer stood in Cissy's way, and that she had never seriously thought of marrying Mr. Bowling. Had she not thought of it? The question did not enter her own mind, and she would have been quite incapable of passing a satisfactory cross-examination on the subject.

Mrs. Mumford, foreseeing the difficulty of spending the next day at home, told her husband in the morning that she would have early luncheon and go to see Mrs. Grove.

'And I should like you to fetch me from there, after business, please.'

'I will,' answered Clarence readily. He mentally added a hope that his wife did not mean to supervise him henceforth and for ever. If so, their troubles were only beginning.

At breakfast, Louise continued to be discretion itself. She talked of her departure on the morrow as though it had long been a settled thing, and was quite unconnected with disagreeable circumstances. Only midway in the morning did Mrs. Mumford, who had been busy with her child, speak of the early luncheon and her journey to town. She hoped Miss Derrick would not mind being left alone.

'Oh, don't speak of it,' answered Louise. 'I've lots to do. You'll give my kind regards to Mrs. Grove?'

So they ate together at midday, rather silently, but with faces composed. And Emmeline, after a last look into the nursery, hastened away to catch her train. She had no misgivings; during her absence, all would be well as ever.

Louise passed the time without difficulty, and at seven o'clock made an excellent dinner. This evening no reply could be expected from Cobb, as he was not likely to have received her letter of last night till his return home from business. Still, there might be something from someone; she always looked eagerly for the postman.

The weather was gloomy. Not long after eight the housemaid brought in a lighted lamp, and set it, as usual, upon the little black four–legged table in the drawing–room. And in the same moment the knocker of the front door sounded a vigorous rat–tat–tat, a visitor's summons.

CHAPTER VIII

'It may be someone calling upon me,' said Louise to the servant. 'Let me know the name before you show anyone in.'

'Of course, miss,' replied the domestic, with pert familiarity, and took her time in arranging the shade of the lamp. When she returned from the door it was to announce, smilingly, that Mr. Cobb wished to see Miss Derrick.

'Please to show him in.'

Louise stood in an attitude of joyous excitement, her eyes sparkling. But at the first glance she perceived that her lover's mood was by no means correspondingly gay. Cobb stalked forward and kept a stern gaze upon her, but said nothing.

'Well? You got my letter, I suppose?'

'What letter?'

He had not been home since breakfast–time, so Louise's appeal to him for advice lay waiting his arrival. Impatiently, she described the course of events. As soon as she had finished, Cobb threw his hat aside and addressed her harshly.

'I want to know what you mean by writing to your sister that you are going to marry Bowling. I saw your mother this morning, and that's what she told me. It must have been only a day or two ago that you said that. Just explain, if you please. I'm about sick of this kind of thing, and I'll have the truth out of you.'

His anger had never taken such a form as this; for the first time Louise did in truth feel afraid of him. She shrank away, her heart throbbed, and her tongue refused its office.

'Say what you mean by it!' Cobb repeated, in a voice that was all the more alarming because he kept it low.

'Did you write that to your sister?'

'Yes — but I never meant it — it was just to make her angry——'

'You expect me to believe that? And, if it's true, doesn't it make you out a nice sort of girl? But I don't believe it You've been thinking of him in that way all along; and you've been writing to him, or meeting him, since you came here. What sort of behaviour do you call this?'

Louise was recovering self–possession; the irritability of her own temper began to support her courage.

'What if I have? I'd never given you any promise till last night, had I? I was free to marry anyone I liked, wasn't I? What do you mean by coming here and going on like this? I've told you the truth about that letter, and I've always told you the truth about everything. If you don't like it, say so and go.'

Cobb was impressed by the energy of her defence. He looked her straight in the eyes, and paused a moment; then spoke less violently.

'You haven't told me the whole truth. I want to know when you saw Bowling last.'

'I haven't seen him since I left home.'

'When did you write to him last?'

'The same day I wrote to Cissy. And I shall answer no more questions.'

'Of course not. But that's quite enough. You've been playing a double game; if you haven't told lies, you've acted them. What sort of a wife would you make? How could I ever believe a word you said? I shall have no more to do with you.'

He turned away, and, in the violence of the movement, knocked over a little toy chair, one of those perfectly useless, and no less ugly, impediments which stand about the floor of a well–furnished drawing–room. Too angry to stoop and set the object on its legs again, he strode towards the door. Louise followed him.

'You are going?' she asked, in a struggling voice.

Cobb paid no attention, and all but reached the door. She laid a hand upon him.

'You are going?'

The touch and the voice checked him. Again he turned abruptly and seized the hand that rested upon his arm.

'Why are you stopping me? What do you want with me? I'm to help you out of the fix you've got into, is that it? I'm to find you a lodging, and take no end of trouble, and then in a week's time get a letter to say that you want nothing more to do with me.'

Louise was pale with anger and fear, and as many other emotions as her little heart and brain could well hold. She did not look her best — far from it but the man saw something in her eyes which threw a fresh spell upon him. Still grasping her one hand, he caught her by the other arm, held her as far off as he could, and glared passionately as he spoke.

'What do you want?'

'You know — I've told you the truth——'

His grasp hurt her; she tried to release herself, and moved backwards. For a moment Cobb left her free; she moved backward again, her eyes drawing him on. She felt her power, and could not be content with thus much exercise of it.

'You may go if you like. But you understand, if you do——'

The Paying Guest

Cobb, inflamed with desire and jealousy, made an effort to recapture her. Louise sprang away from him; but immediately behind her lay the foolish little chair which he had kicked over, and just beyond that stood the scarcely less foolish little table which supported the heavy lamp, with its bowl of coloured glass and its spreading yellow shade. She tottered back, fell with all her weight against the table, and brought the lamp crashing to the floor. A shriek of terror from Louise, from her lover a shout of alarm, blended with the sound of breaking glass. In an instant a great flame shot up half way to the ceiling. The lamp–shade was ablaze; the much–embroidered screen, Mrs. Mumford's wedding present, forthwith caught fire from a burning tongue that ran along the carpet; and Louise's dress, well sprinkled with paraffin, aided the conflagration. Cobb, of course, saw only the danger to the girl. He seized the woollen hearthrug and tried to wrap it about her; but with screams of pain and frantic struggles, Louise did her best to thwart his purpose.

The window was open, and now a servant, rushing in to see what the uproar meant, gave the blaze every benefit of draught.

'Bring water!' roared Cobb, who had just succeeded in extinguishing Louise's dress, and was carrying her, still despite her struggles, out of the room. 'Here, one of you take Miss Derrick to the next house. Bring water, you!'

All three servants were scampering and screeching about the hall. Cobb caught hold of one of them and all but twisted her arm out of its socket. At his fierce command, the woman supported Louise into the garden, and thence, after a minute or two of faintness on the sufferer's part, led her to the gate of the neighbouring house. The people who lived there chanced to be taking the air on their front lawn. Without delay, Louise was conveyed beneath the roof, and her host, a man of energy, sped towards the fire to be of what assistance he could.

The lamp–shade, the screen, the little table and the diminutive chair blazed gallantly, and with such a volleying of poisonous fumes that Cobb could scarce hold his ground to do battle. Louise out of the way, he at once became cool and resourceful. Before a flame could reach the window he had rent down the flimsy curtains and flung them outside. Bellowing for the water which was so long in coming, he used the hearthrug to some purpose on the outskirts of the bonfire, but had to keep falling back for fresh air. Then appeared a pail and a can, which he emptied effectively, and next moment sounded the voice of the gentleman from next door.

The Paying Guest

'Have you a garden hose? Set it on to the tap, and bring it in here.'

The hose was brought into play, and in no great time the last flame had flickered out amid a deluge. When all danger was at an end, one of the servants, the nurse-girl, uttered a sudden shriek; it merely signified that she had now thought for the first time of the little child asleep upstairs. Aided by the housemaid, she rushed to the nursery, snatched her charge from bed, and carried the unhappy youngster into the breezes of the night, where he screamed at the top of his gamut.

Cobb, when he no longer feared that the house would be burnt down, hurried to inquire after Louise. She lay on a couch, wrapped in a dressing-gown; for the side and one sleeve of her dress had been burnt away. Her moaning never ceased; there was a fire-mark on the lower part of her face, and she stared with eyes of terror and anguish at whoever approached her. Already a doctor had been sent for, and Cobb, reporting that all was safe at 'Runnymede,' wished to remove her at once to her own bed room, and the strangers were eager to assist.

'What will the Mumfords say?' Louise asked of a sudden, trying to raise herself.

'Leave all that to me,' Cobb replied reassuringly. 'I'll make it all right; don't trouble yourself.'

The nervous shock had made her powerless; they carried her in a chair back to 'Runnymede,' and upstairs to her bedroom. Scarcely was this done when Mr. and Mrs. Mumford, after a leisurely walk from the station, approached their garden gate. The sight of a little crowd of people in the quiet road, the smell of burning, loud voices of excited servants, caused them to run forward in alarm. Emmeline, frenzied by the certainty that her own house was on fire, began to cry aloud for her child, and Mumford rushed like a madman through the garden.

'It's all right,' said a man who stood in the doorway. 'You Mr. Mumford? It's all right. There's been a fire, but we've got it out.'

Emmeline learnt at the same moment that her child had suffered no harm, but she would not pause until she saw the little one and held him in her embrace. Meanwhile, Cobb and Mumford talked in the devastated drawing-room, which was illumined with candles.

61

The Paying Guest

'It's a bad job, Mr. Mumford. My name is Cobb: I daresay you've heard of me. I came to see Miss Derrick, and I was clumsy enough to knock the lamp over.'

'Knock the lamp over! How could you do that? Were you drunk?'

'No, but you may well ask the question. I stumbled over something — a little chair, I think — and fell against the table with the lamp on it.'

'Where's Miss Derrick?'

'Upstairs. She got rather badly burnt, I'm afraid. We've sent for a doctor.'

'And here I am,' spoke a voice behind them. 'Sorry to see this, Mr. Mumford.'

The two went upstairs together, and on the first landing encountered Emmeline, sobbing and wailing hysterically with the child in her arms. Her husband spoke soothingly.

'Don't, don't, Emmy. Here's Dr. Billings come to see Miss Derrick. She's the only one that has been hurt. Go down, there's a good girl, and send somebody to help in Miss Derrick's room; you can't be any use yourself just now.'

'But how did it happen? Oh, how did it happen?'

'I'll come and tell you all about it. Better put the boy to bed again, hadn't you?'

When she had recovered her senses Emmeline took this advice, and, leaving the nurse by the child's cot, went down to survey the ruin of her property. It was a sorry sight. Where she had left a reception-room such as any suburban lady in moderate circumstances might be proud of; she now beheld a mere mass of unrecognisable furniture, heaped on what had once been a carpet, amid dripping walls and under a grimed ceiling.

'Oh! Oh!' She all but sank before the horror of the spectacle. Then, in a voice of fierce conviction, 'She did it! She did it! It was because I told her to leave. I know she did it on purpose!'

The Paying Guest

Mumford closed the door of the room, shutting out Cobb and the cook and the housemaid. He repeated the story Cobb had told him, and quietly urged the improbability of his wife's explanation. Miss Derrick, he pointed out, was lying prostrate from severe burns; the fire must have been accidental, but the accident, to be sure, was extraordinary enough. Thereupon Mrs. Mumford's wrath turned against Cobb. What business had such a man — a low-class savage — in her drawing-room? He must have come knowing that she and her husband were away for the evening.

'You can question him, if you like,' said Mumford. 'He's out there.'

Emmeline opened the door, and at once heard a cry of pain from upstairs. Mumford, also hearing it, and seeing Cobb's misery-stricken face by the light of the hall lamp, whispered to his wife:

'Hadn't you better go up, dear? Dr. Billings may think it strange.'

It was much wiser to urge this consideration than to make a direct plea for mercy. Emmeline did not care to have it reported that selfish distress made her indifferent to the sufferings of a friend staying in her house. But she could not pass Cobb without addressing him severely.

'So you are the cause of this!'

'I am, Mrs. Mumford, and I can only say that I'll do my best to make good the damage to your house.'

'Make good I fancy you have strange ideas of the value of the property destroyed.'

Insolence was no characteristic of Mrs. Mumford. But calamity had put her beside herself; she spoke, not in her own person, but as a woman whose carpets, curtains and bric-à-brac have ignominiously perished.

'I'll make it good,' Cobb repeated humbly, 'however long it takes me. And don't be angry with that poor girl, Mrs. Mumford. It wasn't her fault, not in any way. She didn't know I was coming; she hadn't asked me to come. I'm entirely to blame.'

The Paying Guest

'You mean to say you knocked over the table by accident?'

'I did indeed. And I wish I'd been burnt myself instead of her.'

He had suffered, by the way, no inconsiderable scorching, to which his hands would testify for many a week; but of this he was still hardly aware. Emmeline, with a glance of uttermost scorn, left him, and ascended to the room where the doctor was busy. Free to behave as he thought fit, Mumford beckoned Cobb to follow him into the front garden, where they conversed with masculine calm.

'I shall put up at Sutton for the night,' said Cobb, 'and perhaps you'll let me call the first thing in the morning to ask how she gets on.'

'Of course. We'll see the doctor when he comes down. But I wish I could understand how you managed to throw the lamp down.'

'The truth is,' Cobb replied, 'we were quarrelling. I'd heard something about her that made me wild, and I came and behaved like a fool. I feel just now as if I could go and cut my throat, that's the fact. If anything happens to her, I believe I shall. I might as well, in any case; she'll never look at me again.'

'Oh, don't take such a dark view of it.'

The doctor came out, on his way to fetch certain requirements, and the two men walked with him to his house in the next road. They learned that Louise was not dangerously injured; her recovery would be merely a matter of time and care. Cobb gave a description of the fire, and his hearers marvelled that the results were no worse.

'You must have some burns too?' said the doctor, whose curiosity was piqued by everything he saw and heard of the strange occurrence. 'I thought so; those hands must be attended to.'

Meanwhile, Emmeline sat by the bedside and listened to the hysterical lamentation in which Louise gave her own — the true — account of the catastrophe. It was all her fault, and upon her let all the blame fall. She would humble herself to Mr. Higgins and get him to pay for the furniture destroyed. If Mrs. Mumford would but forgive her! And so on, as her poor body agonised, and the blood grew feverish in her veins.

CHAPTER VIII

'Accept it? Certainly. Why should we bear the loss if he's able to make it good? He seems to be very well off for an unmarried man.'

'Yes,' replied Mumford, 'but he's just going to marry, and it seems—— Well, after all, you know, he didn't really cause the damage. I should have felt much less scruple if Higgins had offered to pay——'

'He did cause the damage,' asseverated Emmeline. 'It was his gross or violent behaviour. If we had been insured it wouldn't matter so much. And pray let this be a warning, and insure at once. However you look at it, he ought to pay.'

Emmeline's temper had suffered much since she made the acquaintance of Miss Derrick. Aforetime, she could discuss difference of opinion; now a hint of diversity drove her at once to the female weapon — angry and iterative assertion. Her native delicacy, also, seemed to have degenerated. Mumford could only hold his tongue and trust that this would be but a temporary obscurement of his wife's amiable virtues.

Cobb had written from Bristol, a week after the accident, formally requesting a statement of the pecuniary loss which the Mumfords had suffered; he was resolved to repay them, and would do so, if possible, as soon as he knew the sum. Mumford felt a trifle ashamed to make the necessary declaration; at the outside, even with expenses of painting and papering, their actual damage could not be estimated at more than fifty pounds, and even Emmeline did not wish to save appearances by making an excessive demand. The one costly object in the room — the piano — was practically uninjured, and sundry other pieces of furniture could easily be restored; for Cobb and his companion, as amateur firemen, had by no means gone recklessly to work. By candle–light, when the floor was still a swamp, things looked more desperate than they proved to be on subsequent investigation; and it is wonderful at how little outlay, in our glistening times, a villa drawing–room may be fashionably equipped. So Mumford wrote to his correspondent that only a few 'articles' had absolutely perished; that it was not his wish to make any demand at all; but that, if Mr. Cobb insisted on offering restitution, why, a matter of fifty pounds, etc. etc. And in a few days this sum arrived, in the form of a draft upon respectable bankers.

Of course the house was in grievous disorder. Upholsterers' workmen would have been bad enough, but much worse was the establishment of Mrs. Higgins by her daughter's bedside, which naturally involved her presence as a guest at table, and the endurance of her conversation whenever she chose to come downstairs. Mumford urged his wife to take her summer holiday — to go away with the child until all was put right again — a phrase which included the removal of Miss Derrick to her own home; but of this Emmeline would not hear. How could she enjoy an hour of mental quietude when, for all she knew, Mrs. Higgins and the patient might be throwing lamps at each other? And her jealousy was still active, though she did not allow it to betray itself in words. Clarence seemed to her quite needlessly anxious in his inquiries concerning Miss Derrick's condition. Until that young lady had disappeared from 'Runnymede' for ever, Emmeline would keep matronly watch and ward.

Mrs. Higgins declared at least a score of times every day that she could not understand how this dreadful affair had come to pass. The most complete explanation from her daughter availed nothing; she deemed the event an insoluble mystery, and, in familiar talk with Mrs. Mumford, breathed singular charges against Louise's lover. 'She's shielding him, my dear. I've no doubt of it. I never had a very good opinion of him, but now she shall never marry him with my consent.' To this kind of remark Emmeline at length deigned no reply. She grew to detest Mrs. Higgins, and escaped her society by every possible manoeuvre.

'Oh, how pleasant it is,' she explained bitterly to her husband, 'to think that everybody in the road is talking about us with contempt! Of course tile servants have spread nice stories. And the Wilkinsons' — these were the people next door — 'look upon us as hardly respectable. Even Mrs. Fentiman said yesterday that she really could not conceive how I came to take that girl into the house. I acknowledged that I must have been crazy.'

'Whilst we're thoroughly upset,' replied Mumford, with irritation at this purposeless talk, 'hadn't we better leave the house and go to live as far away as possible?'

'Indeed, I very much wish we could. I don't think I shall ever be happy again at Sutton.'

66

The Paying Guest

And Clarence went off muttering to himself about the absurdity and the selfishness of women.

For a week or ten days Louise lay very ill; then her vigorous constitution began to assert itself. It helped her greatly towards convalescence when she found that the scorches on her face would not leave a permanent blemish. Mrs. Mumford came into the room once a day and sat for a few minutes, neither of them desiring longer communion, but they managed to exchange inquiries and remarks with a show of came from Cobb, Emmeline made no friendliness. When the fifty pounds mention of it. The next day, however, Mrs. Higgins being absent when Emmeline looked in, Louise said with an air of satisfaction

'So he has paid the money! I'm very glad of that.'

'Mr. Cobb insisted on paying,' Mrs. Mumford answered with reserve. 'We could not hurt his feelings by refusing.'

'Well, that's all right, isn't it? You won't think so badly of us now? Of course you wish you'd never set eyes on me, Mrs. Mumford; but that's only natural: in your place I'm sure I should feel the same. Still, now the money's paid, you won't always think unkindly of me, will you?'

The girl lay propped on pillows; her pale face, with its healing scars, bore witness to what she had undergone, and. one of her arms was completely swathed in bandages. Emmeline did not soften towards her, but the frank speech, the rather pathetic little smile, in decency demanded a suave response.

'I shall wish you every happiness, Louise.'

'Thank you. We shall be married as soon as ever I'm well, but I'm sure I don't know where. Mother hates his very name, and does her best to set me against him; but I just let her talk. We're beginning to quarrel a little — did you hear us this morning? I try to keep down my voice, and I shan't be here much longer, you know. I shall go home at first my stepfather has written a kind letter, and of course he's glad to know I shall marry Mr. Cobb. But I don't think the wedding will be there. It wouldn't be nice to go to church in a rage, as I'm sure I should with mother and Cissy looking on.'

This might, or might not, signify a revival of the wish to be married from 'Runnymede.' Emmeline quickly passed to another subject.

Mrs. Higgins was paying a visit to Coburg Lodge, where, during the days of confusion, the master of the house had been left at his servants' mercy. On her return, late in the evening, she entered flurried and perspiring, and asked the servant who admitted her where Mrs. Mumford was.

'With master, in the library, 'm.'

'Tell her I wish to speak to her at once.'

Emmeline came forth, and a lamp was lighted in the dining–room, for the drawing–room had not yet been restored to a habitable condition. Silent, and wondering in gloomy resignation what new annoyance was prepared for her, Emmeline sat with eyes averted, whilst the stout woman mopped her face and talked disconnectedly of the hardships of travelling in such weather as this; when at length she reached her point, Mrs. Higgins became lucid and emphatic.

'I've heard things as have made me that angry I can hardly bear myself. Would you believe that people are trying to take away my daughter's character? It's Cissy 'Iggins's doing: I'm sure of it, though I haven't brought it 'ome to her yet. I dropped in to see some friends of ours — I shouldn't wonder if you know the name; it's Mrs. Jolliffe, a niece of Mr. Baxter — Baxter, Lukin and Co., you know. And she told me in confidence what people are saying — as how Louise was to marry Mr. Bowling, but he broke it off when he found the sort of people she was living with, here at Sutton — and a great many more things as I shouldn't like to tell you. Now what do you think of——'

Emmeline, her eyes flashing, broke in angrily:

'I think nothing at all about it, Mrs. Higgins, and I had very much rather not hear the talk of such people.'

'I don't wonder it aggravates you, Mrs. Mumford. Did anyone ever hear such a scandal! I'm sure nobody that knows you could say a word against your respectability, and, as I told Mrs. Jolliffe, she's quite at liberty to call here to–morrow or the next day——'

The Paying Guest

'Not to see me, I hope,' said Emmeline. 'I must refuse——'

'Now just let me tell you what I've thought,' pursued the stout lady, hardly aware of this interruption. 'This'll have to be set right, both for Lou's sake and for yours, and to satisfy us all. They're making a mystery, d'you see, of Lou leaving 'ome and going off to live with strangers; and Cissy's been doing her best to make people think there's something wrong — the spiteful creature! And there's only one way of setting it right. As soon as Lou can be dressed and got down, and when the drawing–room's finished, I want her to ask all our friends here to five o'clock tea, just to let them see with their own eyes——'

'Mrs. Higgins!'

'Of course there'll be no expense for you, Mrs. Mumford — not a farthing. I'll provide everything, and all I ask of you is just to sit in your own drawing–room——'

'Mrs. Higgins, be so kind as to listen to me. This is quite impossible. I can't dream of allowing any such thing.'

The other glared in astonishment, which tended to wrath.

'But can't you see, Mrs. Mumford, that it's for your own good as well as ours? Do you want people to be using your name——'

'What can it matter to me how such people think or speak of me?' cried Emmeline, trembling with exasperation.

'Such people! I don't think you know who you're talking about, Mrs. Mumford. You'll let me tell you that my friends are as respectable as yours——'

'I shall not argue about it,' said Emmeline, standing up. 'You will please to remember that already I've had a great deal of trouble and annoyance, and what you propose would be quite intolerable. Once for all, I can't dream of such a thing.'

'Then all I can say is, Mrs. Mumford' — the speaker rose with heavy dignity — 'that you're not behaving in a very ladylike way. I'm not a quarrelsome person, as you well know, and I don't say nasty things if I can help it. But there's one thing I must say and will say, and that is, that when we first came here you gave a very different account of yourself to what it's turned out. You told me and my daughter distinctly that you had a great deal of the very best society, and that was what Lou came here for, and you knew it, and you can't deny that you did. And I should like to know how much society she's seen all the time she's been here — that's the question I ask you. I don't believe she's seen more than three or four people altogether. They may have been respectable enough, and I'm not the one to say they weren't, but I do say it isn't what we was led to expect, and that you can't deny, Mrs. Mumford.'

She paused for breath. Emmeline had moved towards the door, and stood struggling with the feminine rage which impelled her to undignified altercation. To withdraw in silence would be like a shamed confession of the charge brought against her, and she suffered not a little from her consciousness of the modicum of truth therein.

'It was a most unfortunate thing, Mrs. Higgins,' burst from her lips, 'that I ever consented to receive your daughter, knowing as I did that she wasn't our social equal.'

'Wasn't what?' exclaimed the other, as though the suggestion startled her by its novelty. 'You think yourself superior to us? You did us a favour——'

Whilst Mrs. Higgins was uttering these words the door opened, and there entered a figure which startled her into silence. It was that of Louise, in a dressing–gown and slippers, with a shawl wrapped about the upper part of her body.

'I heard you quarrelling,' she began. (Her bedroom was immediately above, and at this silent hour the voices of the angry ladies had been quite audible to her as she lay in bed.) 'What is it all about? It's too bad of you, mother——'

'The idea, Louise, of coming down like that!' cried her parent indignantly. 'How did you know Mr. Mumford wasn't here? For shame! Go up again this moment.'

'I don't see any harm if Mr. Mumford had been here,' replied the girl calmly.

'I'm sure it's most unwise of you to leave your bed,' began Emmeline, with anxious thought for Louise's health, due probably to her dread of having the girl in the house for an indefinite period.

The Paying Guest

'Oh, I've wrapped up. I feel shaky, that's all, and I shall have to sit down.' She did so, on the nearest chair, with a little laugh at her strange feebleness.

'Now please don't quarrel, you two. Mrs. Mumford, don't mind anything that mother says.'

Thereupon Louise's mother burst into a vehement exposition of the reasons of discord, beginning with the calumnious stories she had heard at Mrs. Jolliffe's, and ending with the outrageous arrogance of Mrs. Mumford's latest remark. Louise listened with a smile.

'Now look here, mother,' she said, when silence came for a moment, 'you can't expect Mrs. Mumford to have a lot of strangers coming to the house just on my account. She's sick and tired of us all, and wants to see our backs as soon as ever she can. I don't say it to offend you, Mrs. Mumford, but you know it's true. And I tell you what it is: To—morrow morning I'm going back home. Yes, I am. You can't stay here, mother, after this, and I'm not going to have anyone new to wait on me. I shall go home in a cab, straight from this house to the other, and I'm quite sure I shan't take any harm.'

'You won't do it till the doctor's given you leave,' said Mrs. Higgins with concern.

'He'll be here at ten in the morning, and I know he will give me leave. So there's an end of it. And you can go to bed and sleep in peace, Mrs. Mumford.'

It was not at all unamiably said. But for Mrs. Higgins's presence, Emmeline would have responded with a certain kindness. Still smarting under the stout lady's accusations, which continued to sound in sniffs and snorts, she answered as austerely as possible.

'I must leave you to judge, Miss Derrick, how soon you feel able to go. I don't wish you to do anything imprudent. But it will be much better if Mrs. Higgins regards me as a stranger during the rest of her stay here. Any communication she wishes to make to me must be made through a servant.'

Having thus delivered herself; Emmeline quitted the room. From the library, of which the door was left ajar, she heard Louise and her mother pass upstairs, both silent. Mumford, too well aware that yet another disturbance had come upon his unhappy household, affected to read, and it was only when the door of Louise's room had closed that

The Paying Guest

Emmeline spoke to him.

'Mrs. Higgins will breakfast by herself to-morrow,' she said severely. 'She may perhaps go before lunch; but in any case we shall not sit down at table with her again.'

'All right,' Mumford replied, studiously refraining from any hint of curiosity.

So, next morning, their breakfast was served in the library. Mrs. Higgins came down at the usual hour, found the dining-room at her disposal, and ate with customary appetite, alone. Had Emmeline's experience lain among the more vigorously vulgar of her sex she would have marvelled at Mrs. Higgins's silence and general self-restraint during these last hours. Louise's mother might, without transgressing the probabilities of the situation, have made this a memorable morning indeed. She confined herself to a rather frequent ringing of the bedroom bell. Her requests of the servants became orders, such as she would have given in a hotel or lodging-house, but no distinctly offensive word escaped her. And this was almost entirely due to Louise's influence for the girl impressed upon her mother that 'to make a row' would be the sure and certain way of proving that Mrs. Mumford was justified in claiming social superiority over her guests.

The doctor, easily perceiving how matters stood, made no difficulty about the patient's removal in a closed carriage, and, with exercise of all obvious precautions, she might travel as soon as she liked. Anticipating this, Mrs. Higgins had already packed all the luggage, and Louise, as well as it could be managed, had been clad for the journey.

'I suppose you'll go and order the cab yourself?' she said to her mother, when they were alone again.

'Yes, I must, on account of making a bargain about the charge. A nice expense you've been to us, Louise. That man ought to pay every penny.'

'I'll tell him you say so, and no doubt he will.'

They wrangled about this whilst Mrs. Higgins was dressing to go out. As soon as her mother had left the house Louise stole downstairs and to the door of the drawing-room, which was half open. Emmeline, her back turned, stood before the fireplace, as if considering some new plan of decoration; she did not hear the girl's light step.

The Paying Guest

Whitewashers and paperhangers had done their work; a new carpet was laid down; but pictures had still to be restored to their places, and the furniture stood all together in the middle of the room. Not till Louise had entered did her hostess look round.

'Mrs. Mumford, I want to say good–bye.'

'Oh, yes,' Emmeline answered civilly, but without a smile. 'Good–bye, Miss Derrick.'

And she stepped forward to shake hands.

'Don't be afraid,' said the girl, looking into her face good–humouredly. 'You shall never see me again unless you wish to.'

'I'm sure I wish you all happiness,' was the embarrassed reply. 'And — I shall be glad to hear of your marriage.'

'I'll write to you about it. But you won't talk — unkindly about me when I've gone — you and Mr. Mumford?'

'No, no; indeed we shall not.'

Louise tried to say something else, but without success. She pressed Emmeline's hand, turned quickly, and disappeared. In half–an–hour's time arrived the vehicle Mrs. Higgins had engaged; without delay mother and daughter left the house, and were driven off. Mrs. Mumford kept a strict retirement. When the two had gone she learnt from the housemaid that their luggage would be removed later in the day.

A fortnight passed, and the Mumfords once more lived in enjoyment of tranquillity, though Emmeline could not quite recover her old self. They never spoke of the dread experiences through which they had gone. Mumford's holiday time approached, and they were making arrangements for a visit to the seaside, when one morning a carrier's cart delivered a large package, unexpected and of unknown contents. Emmeline stripped off the matting, and found — a drawing–room screen, not unlike that which she had lost in the fire. Of course it came from Louise, and, though she professed herself very much annoyed, Mrs. Mumford had no choice but to acknowledge it in a civil little note addressed to Coburg Lodge.

The Paying Guest

They were away from home for three weeks. On returning, Emmeline found a letter which had arrived for her the day before; it was from Louise, and announced her marriage. 'Dear Mrs. Mumford, — I know you'll be glad to hear it's all over. It was to have been at the end of October, when our house was ready for us. We have taken a very nice one at Holloway. But of course something happened, and mother and Cissy and I quarrelled so dreadfully that I went off and took a lodging. And then Tom said that we must be married at once; and so we were, without any fuss at all, and I think it was ever so much better, though some girls would not care to go in their plain dress and without friends or anything. After it was over, Tom and I had just a little disagreement about something, but of course he gave way, and I don't think we shall get on together at all badly. My stepfather has been very nice, and is paying for all the furniture, and has promised me a lot of things. Of course he is delighted to see me out of the house, just as you were. You see that I write from Broadstairs, where we are spending our honeymoon. Please remember me to Mr. Mumford, and believe me, very sincerely yours, Louise L. Cobb.'

Enclosed was a wedding–card. 'Mr. and Mrs. Thomas Cobb,' in gilt lettering, occupied the middle, and across the right–hand upper corner ran 'Louise E. Derrick,' an arrow transfixing the maiden surname.

Printed in the United Kingdom
by Lightning Source UK Ltd.
106665UKS00002B/192

9 781419 176906